Walter Bell Scaife

America

its geographical history 1492-1892 - six lectures delivered to graduate students of

the Johns Hopkins University

Walter Bell Scaife

America
its geographical history 1492-1892 - six lectures delivered to graduate students of the Johns Hopkins University

ISBN/EAN: 9783337399788

Printed in Europe, USA, Canada, Australia, Japan

Cover: Foto ©Andreas Hilbeck / pixelio.de

More available books at **www.hansebooks.com**

AMERICA

ITS GEOGRAPHICAL HISTORY

1492-1892

Six Lectures delivered to Graduate Students of
the Johns Hopkins University

WITH A

SUPPLEMENT

ENTITLED

WAS THE RIO DEL ESPÍRITU SANTO OF THE SPAN-
ISH GEOGRAPHERS THE MISSISSIPPI?

By WALTER B. SCAIFE, Ph. D. (Vienna)

———————

BALTIMORE
THE JOHNS HOPKINS PRESS
1892

JOHN MURPHY & CO, PRINTERS,
BALTIMORE.

CONTENTS.

LIST OF MAPS.

1. American portion of Juan de la Coza's map of the world, 1500; from Jomard.
2. The Cantino map, from Harrisse.
3. The Ruysch map, 1508; from original in Astor Library.
4. Spanish official map of 1527; from original in Grand-Ducal Library, Weimar.
5. Ribero's map, 1529; from original also in Weimar.
6. Portion of America, Cabot's map of 1544; from Jomard.
7. Portion of Mercator's map of the world, 1569; from Jomard.
8. America according to Ortelius, 1570; from original in Astor Library.
9. Hennepin's map; from English Edition, 1699.
10. Thomas Hood's map, 1592; from original MS. in Royal Library, Munich. Described in Codices Manuscripti Bibliothecae Regiae Monacensis, by Georgius M. Thomas. Munich, 1858, pp. 272–273.

To my friend and former instructor, Professor Herbert B. Adams, to whose kindness these lectures owe their origin, this book is affectionately dedicated by

The Author.

NOTE.

The author takes pleasure in acknowledging the debt of gratitude he owes to Professor T. C. Mendenhall, Director of the U. S. Coast and Geodetic Survey; to Mr. Henry Gannett, Chief Topographer of the U. S. Geological Survey; and to Mr. Frederic Bancroft, late Librarian of the Library of the Department of State, for their kind assistance rendered in the prosecution of his work. His thanks are also due to the librarians of the Grand-Ducal Library at Weimar, of the Royal Library at Munich, of the Astor Library, and of the American Geographical Society in New York, for the privilege of having photographed valuable maps in their keeping.

PHILADELPHIA,
March, 1892.

AMERICA: ITS GEOGRAPHICAL HISTORY.

I.

THE DEVELOPMENT OF THE ATLANTIC COAST IN THE CONSCIOUSNESS OF EUROPE.

It is proposed in this lecture to give an outline of the manner in which a knowledge of the Atlantic coast-line of America
grew into the consciousness of the Europeans. For this purpose it is not necessary to go back to the time of the Northmen,
though there is no reasonable room for doubt that they, centuries
before Columbus, discovered and occupied a portion of North
America. But their settlements died out, and the knowledge
of their discoveries failed to penetrate civilized Europe. Our
theme begins in the night from the 11th to the 12th of October, 1492. Picture to yourselves Columbus anxiously walking
the deck of his diminutive hundred-ton ship, at ten o'clock at
night, in the moonlight, and wondering if he would ever see
the shores of the golden India, of which he had dreamed and
talked for so many years. Suddenly a strange light appears
on the horizon. The heart of the watcher beats wildly. Surely
that betokens the presence of man ; and not far off, there must
be land. How slowly the minutes pass as his anxious eyes peer
into the gray moonlight, searching for a glimpse of land. But
four long hours go by before the low-lying coast can be dis-
cerned. The ship then casts anchor, and its occupants await

1

the day.   They were off a little island which the natives called
Guanahani.   Here American geography begins ; and from
this little island it expanded, in the course of a couple of
centuries, to include two vast continents.

This island of Guanahani plays a great part in the history of
American discovery, as the first point touched by the foot of
the fifteenth century explorer ; and accordingly it will be worth
our while to consider for a few moments the various theories
that have been advanced to establish the claim of one island
or another to the proud title of the first discovery on this
western shore.

The difficulties in the way of solving the problem are great.
The description of Columbus that has come down to our time
is meagre, and the then state of scientific knowledge was such
that we cannot now rely absolutely on the data of his log of
the voyage.   Here he took no observation as to his latitude ;
and even if he had done so it might have resulted in showing
him as far from arriving at his true position as it did a little
later when he tried to get his latitude near the north-western
point of the present Hayti, and found it to be in latitude 17,
when in fact it is almost 20 degrees north of the equator.   In
his journal we find in reference to Guanahani the following :
" This island is very [better, quite] large and very level and
has very green trees, and abundance of water, and a very large
lagoon in the middle, without any mountain, and all is covered
with verdu[r]e, most pleasing to the eye." "At dawn I ordered
the boat of the ship and the boats of the Caravels to be got
ready, and went along the island, in a north-northeasterly
direction, to see the other side, which was on the other side of
the east.—But I was afraid of a reef of rocks which entirely
surrounds that island, although there is within it depth enough
and ample harbor for all the vessels of Christendom, but the
entrance is very narrow.   It is true that the interior of that
belt contains some rocks [Spanish bajas, or shallows], but the
sea is there as still as the water in a well.   And in order to see
all this I moved this morning, that I might give an account "

"of everything to your Highnesses, and also to see where a fort could be built, and found a piece of land like an island, although it is not one, with six houses on it, which in two days could easily be cut off and converted into an island." . . . "I observed all that harbor, and afterwards I returned to the ship and set sail, and saw so many islands that I could not decide to which one I should go first, and the men I had taken told me by signs that they were innumerable, and named more than one hundred of them."[1] As the islands of the Bahama group are so numerous, and the magnetical data of the log of the voyage so uncertain, various interpretations of the meagre facts known to us have accordingly been made; and thus no less than five different islands are respectively asserted to be the original Guanahani. These are Grand Turk, advocated especially by the Spanish historian Navarrete; 2, Marignana, resulting from the researches of the Dutch investigator Varnhagen; 3, Watling's Island, adopted by Muñoz, Becher, Major; 4, Cat Island, which received the recognition of von Humboldt and Washington Irving. The last one, Samana, is advocated with great elaborateness by Captain G. V. Fox of the United States navy, who, at the request of the national government, made an exhaustive study of the whole subject; not only theoretically but also practically, going over the entire section of the West Indies in question, and examining the topography of the several islands, their relative positions, etc.

The last word comes from a German source, Mr. Rudolf Cronau, who made a tour of investigation in the autumn of 1890, and leaving aside the log of Columbus, looked only to his description of the island itself and his course after leaving it until he reached Cuba. To these points he adds the remark of Las Casas, that "the first land was one of those islands which we call the Lucayos. The said island has the form of a bean." His conclusion is, "that Guanahani is solely and alone

---

[1] Translation in Capt. Fox's *Methods and Results.*

with Watling's Island identical, and that Columbus landed on the west side of this island." And with this conclusion the weight of modern authority is in harmony.

Watling's Island, Mr. Cronau informs us, is the only one of the group, that has the form of a bean, excepting New Providence, which does not enter into the question ; further, that it has a large salt-water lake in the interior, such as Columbus described, and that there is nothing in the nature of a mountain on the island, as the ridges that divide the lagoons are but 100 to 140 feet high ; also, that vegetation here corresponds so well with the praise of its first discoverer, that the island is to this day known as "the garden of the Bahamas." He is of the opinion that Columbus must have discovered the island, coming from the north, and landed at a point now called Riding Rocks, where there is a settlement of the name of Cockburn Town. Elsewhere surrounding the island is a reef, with a very narrow entrance, with here and there shallows, but which nevertheless encloses an open space that would be large enough to accommodate large fleets, just as it appears in Columbus' description. Finally, the northeast point of the island corresponds exactly with the idea of a place for a fortification, described by the Admiral ; and in fact Cronau found here a cannon, evidently of the last century, which shows that others have seen how well this point was adapted to the defense of the island.

As to the early cartographical representations of the island, it stands on the chart of Juan de la Cosa, the earliest map of America that we possess, very nearly in the same relation to Cuba and Hayti as Watling's Island does on the modern maps. However, the neighboring small islands on this map do not agree in form and situation with modern charts, so that we cannot consider the evidence of Cosa as of much weight. But the celebrated Spanish official maps of 1527 and 1529 respectively, which are in the grand-ducal library of Weimar, show the island of Guanahani conspicuously drawn in the form of a cross with a number of small dots around it. The position

of this island on these maps in relation to Cuba, Hayti, Great
Bahama, and other neighboring islands, agrees so well with
that of Watling's Island on modern maps, that there is little
room for reasonable doubt, that the makers thereof believed
Guanahani to be in the position of the island now known as
Watling's. When it is considered that these maps were made
in Spain, by the official cartographers, within 35 and 37 years
of the original discovery, at a time when they would probably
be exposed to the criticism of men who knew the island personally, it seems extremely probable that Guanahani and
Watling's Island are one and the same.

Leaving Guanahani, Columbus next visited several other
small islands in the vicinity, and after ten days reached Cuba.
It was probably at Nipe Bay that he first sighted this great
island, whence he coasted some distance to the northwest, then
turned back and pursued a southeasterly course till he reached
the eastern extremity of the island, from which point he could
see the opposite heights of Hayti, toward which he directed
his little fleet. Here was to be made, later, the first attempt
in modern times to found a European colony in the Western
Hemisphere; here was to be the commencement of American
political geography. Sailing to the east, he sighted the island
of Tortuga, but clung to the coast of Hayti as far as the
present bay of Samana, where he halted for trade with the
Indians; thence he followed the coast far enough to the east
and south to convince himself that the body of land was an
island. Columbus returned thence home, to spread abroad
the news of his discovery. Arrived at the Spanish court,
he gave a detailed description of his voyage, and asked for
assistance to prosecute his discoveries further. American
geography, then, in the spring of 1493, consisted of Columbus's chart and description of some newly found islands in the
far off west, which islands were believed to be near India.

The province of geography is not, however, to follow the
fate of individuals in their wanderings; but rather, in our
case, to gather up the results of those western voyages which

opened up some new territory to the consciousness of Europe, or rendered more accurate the knowledge of that previously discovered ; and also to see how this knowledge became spread abroad throughout Christendom.   Travellers are usually fond of relating their adventures, and it is easy for them to procure an audience.   Furthermore, for such an important subject as the discovery of a New World, which title soon came into use, there were those only too happy to write down the narratives with which they were entertained.   Then too the explorers themselves had often to make report of results to those furnishing the means of prosecuting the work.   In the case of Spain these reports were preserved in a special bureau established for the purpose, by an ordinance of January 20th, 1503. It bore the name of " *Casa de la Contratacion de las Indias* ; " and its records now form one of the most valuable sources of our knowledge of the early explorations.   Moreover, there were the cosmographers, whose work now began to assume an importance, previously unknown ; while the then newly invented art of printing added greatly in dispersing throughout Europe a knowledge of the discoveries made by the representatives of the various countries.   News-letters and pamphlets took the place of the present daily papers ; and a book that became popular in one language was very likely to be translated into others.   The information thus conveyed was often far from correct ; and many fables were thereby circulated in regard to the wonders of the New World.

On his return from the first voyage, Columbus landed first in Portugal, where the news of his discoveries was soon noised abroad.   In Spain, he came in contact with Peter Martyr, who wrote letters on the discoveries to various great personages in Italy.   In September of the same year, 1493, the queen demands of Columbus a chart of his voyage, which is delivered ; and this, or a later one, came into the hands of Ojeda, an enemy of Columbus, who used it in 1499 during the latter's absence in the New World, to direct his course to the west, in the attempt to outdo Columbus in his own field.

To Genoa, news of the discovery was soon carried by the ambassadors Marchesi and Grimaldi. In March, 1494, the government of Florence received written notices of the discovery in the great ocean, of islands where the Spaniards had found naked inhabitants, who gave for a pin gold to the value of several ducats. In the following month of June, the subject was mentioned in an important public address in Rome. During his third voyage, Columbus forwarded to Spain a map of the coast of South America just discovered; and there is a report of his having sent a map to the pope the same year; but whether it was a copy of the last-mentioned or an entirely different map, we are not informed. The Venetian government, about the same time, ordered its ambassadors to make special efforts to procure information concerning the new discoveries; and they accordingly approached Columbus and Peter Martyr for the purpose of acquiring maps and accurate descriptions of the lands discovered.

From Spain and its discoveries in the south, we turn for a moment to England and the exploration of the north. Although a recent writer says : "The credit of being the first to explore our Atlantic coast has not yet been positively awarded by critical historians," yet we are disposed to accept for our geographical purposes the generally accredited account of Cabot's discovery of the coast of North America in the year 1497. His landfall was probably Cape Breton or thereabouts. During that and subsequent voyages, Sebastian Cabot, who at first accompanied his father and was afterwards commander, explored with more or less accuracy the eastern coast of the western continent from $67\frac{1}{2}$ degrees north, southward, perhaps as far as Chesapeake Bay. He was the first to propose a northwest passage to Cathay, the name of China then usual in Europe, on the ground that by the adoption of what is now known as great circle sailing, one would take the shortest route thither. Cabot's exploring activity continued many years, in the service of Spain and England, and he is supposed to have died in the latter country about 1557. It was chiefly through him that Great Britain derived its claim, by right of discovery, to the Atlantic seaboard of North America. In the meantime, others had visited the eastern coast, of whose voyages we possess no detailed accounts, but of which early maps seem to have preserved to us evidence of the actuality of their knowledge.

The investigations of M. Harrisse have brought to light the fact that the Portuguese were, at a very early period, certainly before 1502, on the eastern coast of North America ; for he not only finds evidence thereof in contemporary letters, but also undeniable proof in the Cantino map, which he has edited and published in facsimile. This is a very large map which was carried in that year from Portugal to Ercole d'Este, duke of Ferrara, by a man named Cantino, whose function in Portugal is not known. On this map the southern portion of Greenland is quite well depicted ; and to the southwest thereof is drawn a coast-line which is probably that of Newfoundland, though its position is very far to the east. Apparently unmistakable is the coast of Florida, and its extensions to the north on the Atlantic sea-board and to the west on the Gulf of Mexico. But opinion on the subject is much divided, some authorities seeing therein only a repetition of Cuba, arising from a misunderstanding of Spanish accounts of the discoveries in the western hemisphere. All authorities agree, however, that this is the type if not original of many of the later maps known to us.

The southern part of the continent, however, was destined to be brought earlier than the northern into more accurate knowledge of the Europeans; so we ask again attention to that portion. There exists indeed a map of the fourteenth century, made by an Italian, a certain Zeno, who passed some time in Iceland and the far north, on which is portrayed what is supposed to be a portion of North America, according to the ideas or knowledge of the Icelanders. But as this map was not made known to the public till the middle of the sixteenth century, we may pass it by, and turn to the oldest map known to us on which is given a representation of America as it was actually known. This is the map of Juan de la Cosa, one of the companions of Columbus; and bears the date 1500. The original is a large map of the then known world, drawn on an oxhide, with elaborate gilding and coloring, and is still preserved at Madrid. The western portion gives the results of Spanish explorations up to that date. It represents also the eastern coast of North America to a considerable extent, but trending entirely too much to the east. The northern line of South America is also given, and that naturally with greater accuracy than the other, as it was the part known directly by the Spaniards, while they probably knew only by report, of Cabot's discovery in the north. Between the northern and southern portions, the only connection is by means of a vignette; for that portion of the continent was as yet unknown; and a tradition later spread abroad that a strait existed there, leading to oriental waters. No general name is given to all the new lands discovered, for it was still believed that they were a part of Asia. The principal north and south line is marked "*Lina Meridional*," and is intended to represent the line of demarcation which had been agreed upon between Spain and Portugal, in their famous division of the then unexplored world. It passes through the northeastern part of North America, and cuts off a small corner of South America. The equator and tropics are also given; but so faulty was the knowledge of latitude that Cuba and Hayti, are both placed entirely north of the Tropic of Cancer, although, in fact both are entirely south of it. We are not accustomed to think that by the year 1500 the Spaniards knew much, if anything, of the coast of North America; yet on this map there are no less than seventeen names there, a fact which shows that Cosa already had some knowledge of the English voyages to the New World. The interior, of which nothing was known, is ornamented with lakes and rivers thrown in *ad libitum*. The coast of South America is supplied with many names, some of which are still in use.

(Mr. Winsor, speaking of the original, says there are 45 names here.) Among others we find " C. de la Vela," a name now borne by a city in the same neighborhood ; " Venezueda," which is none other than the modern Venezuela or little Venice ; and was so named in 1499 by Ojeda, because the houses were built on piles in a manner that reminded him of Venice.   Here is also " I. de Brasil," a name afterwards trans-ferred to the whole Portuguese possessions on the mainland. The island now known as Hayti and San Domingo bears the name "La Espagnola," conferred upon it by Columbus because its landscape reminded him much of Spain.   Nine local names are on it, one of which is Domingo, on the southeastern coast, the name now used to designate the whole eastern half of the island ; while the name Hayti, now applied to the western portion of the island, occurs on the map under consideration in the form " Haiti," which means " mountainous country," and designates a small island lying to the north of " La Espagnola." The name Guanahani is here given to a small outlying island, with Samana south of it.   The island of Cuba[1] receives its present name on this map, although Columbus had called it Iuana.

La Cosa's representation of Cuba has given rise to much discussion, in as much as Columbus, on his second voyage, required from his companions an oath to the effect that they believed it to be a part of the main land.   On this map, how-ever, it is distinctly represented as an island.   Mr. Stevens contended that the western portion is in green, a color used by La Cosa to designate unknown land.   In the fac-simile of Jomard,[2] in the Astor Library of New York, the color of the western portion is not at all different from that of the rest of

---

[1] Mr. Winsor in *Nar. and Crit. Hist.*, II, 182-3, falls into the error of ascribing the first use of this name as designating that island to the "Cos-mographicus liber " of Apianus, published in 1524.

[2] Mr. Stevens himself acknowledges that he, "the writer, has never had under his eye the original chart, but judges only from Mr. Jomard's excel-lent colored fac-simile." Notes, p. 34, note.

the island, and is a yellowish-brown, with no resemblance to the green of the unknown interior of the mainland. Moreover, not only is a western coast-line distinctly drawn, but still further to the west are other islands intervening between this coast and the mainland. Now La Cosa had subscribed to the oath, and had even added that he had never heard "of any island 335 leagues long, and hence he believed Cuba to be in Asia" (*Ibid.*, p. 12). But the Indians had told Columbus on his first voyage that it was an island; and there is every possibility of Cosa's having changed his mind between 1494, when he subscribed to that oath, and 1500 when he drew the map, particularly as he had in the meantime made another voyage to the New World. Officially, Cuba was not circumnavigated before the year 1508; yet Mr. Winsor has, in his recent work on Columbus, expressed the opinion that its insularity was perhaps previously known, notwithstanding the vigorous protest against that view published by Mr. Stevens and seconded by Mr. Coote. The latter, of the British Museum, in his introduction to Stevens on Schoener, makes merry at the credulity of Mr. Harrisse, Mr. Winsor and others, who interpret the Cantino map and similar ones as evidence of the existence of any knowledge of the mainland of Florida before its discovery by Ponce de Leon; for he himself sees therein only a "bogus Cuba," invented by the Portuguese from a misunderstanding of the facts as reported from Spain; and, as Spain tried to keep her knowledge to herself, and the Portuguese were free to spread broadcast their maps of Spanish possessions in the New World, the latter became known and largely copied throughout Europe, thus disseminating false ideas which it took a long time to eradicate. Mr. Coote finds strong confirmatory evidence of his theory in the fact that these maps transfer more or less of the names that Columbus applied to Cuba, to what appears to represent the mainland. However, that does not alter the fact that Cosa himself depicts Cuba distinctly as an island. His mainland is indeed different from that drawn by Cantino

and other representatives of the Portuguese idea; but he doubtless intended to represent that mainland as part of Asia.
We have seen how England soon followed in the wake of the Spaniards to the New World. In the year 1500 the Portuguese navigator Cabral reached the coast of South America, driven thither perhaps by adverse winds, or seeking a lost ship of his fleet, or going so far to the west merely to avoid the prevailing winds on the coast of Africa,—for all these differing opinions are held by various writers. As early as 1503 the French also reached the coast of Brazil; in 1504 they commenced fishing near Newfoundland; and as early as 1506 their hardy sailors had gained a knowledge of the Gulf of St. Lawrence, which was embodied in a map by one Denys, of Honfleur. Thus the sixteenth century opens with the maritime nations of Europe full of curiosity as to the New World, and possessed of bold navigators ready and anxious to do all in their power to explore its mysteries. The Atlantic became a great highway; and almost every year saw new expeditions sent forth in search of wealth and fame. The Spaniards extended their explorations both to the north and south; the English found it expedient on the whole to confine themselves to the north; though they did not hesitate to make piratical cruises against Spanish ships returning to the mother country laden with the spoils of the west; the French essayed explorations along almost the entire Atlantic coast of the western continent, meeting with opposition wherever they went,—on the north from the English, on the south from the Spanish. The curiosity of all Christendom had been aroused as to the discoveries made in the New World; but each exploring nation endeavored to keep its knowledge to itself. Accordingly we find that the best dispersers of this knowledge were the non-exploring nations,—the Italians, the Germans, and later the Dutch. The first book containing a collection of voyages, of which a copy is known to exist, was made by a Venetian diplomate in Spain, Angelo Trivigiano, who translated several reports of voyages, collected letters, and pub-

lished them all together in the year 1507. Within a year afterwards two translations of the same were published, a Latin one in Milan and a German one in Nuremberg.

In the 1508 edition of Ptolemy there is a map of the world, thought by Humboldt to be the work of Johann Ruysch. It is in the form of an open fan, representing somewhat more than a quarter circle. The north pole is at the apex, while the outer rim represents about the 38th degree of south latitude. The then known coast of North America is attached to the north-east of Asia; here the name " In. Baccalauras," a designation often given to Newfoundland, is applied to a diminutive island, in a bay enclosed by "C. de Portugesi," which cape forms the extremity of a long peninsula bearing the name " Terra nova." Thence the coast-line trends to the west, and connects with " Gog," " Magog," and other places bearing names at that time given to portions of Asia. East of the mainland, there extends from a scroll a broad land on which there are half a dozen names not now in use. Of South America only the north and east coasts are given. The region bears the legend: " Terra Sanctae Crucis Sive Mundus Novus." Among other names on the north coast, we find " Terr. de Pareas " and " Golfo de Pareas," names probably conferred by Columbus himself. Mr. Winsor remarks that " it is thought that Ruysch used Columbus' draughts." " Rio Grande " is probably meant for the Orinoco. The "Jordan " river finds place just south of the Tropic of Capricorn, a name long borne by the present Rio de la Plata. An inscription says " Nauti Lusitani " had penetrated to 50° S. without finding the southern extremity of the land. Among the islands we find the names: "Spagnola," " Le XI Mil Virgines," " Martinina," " La Dominica," and " Antillia Insula."

In 1512 there was published in Cracow, the ancient capital of Poland, an edition of the Geography of Ptolemy which contains a map of the world, on which America finds place. The map is drawn in a network of meridians and parallels at intervals of ten degrees, and the tropics also are added. This

is one of those maps before alluded to, which are open to
discussion as to whether what appears to be Florida and the
mainland of America are not a duplicate Cuba. The name
" isabello," which really belonged to Cuba, and is here placed
on what seems to be Florida, certainly tends to confirm Mr.
Coote's idea. Another feature of these maps is that they
represent the supposed Florida as entirely west of the longitude
of Cuba, instead of north of its western part, as it in reality
is. Of South America, the northern and eastern portions are
fairly well represented, while the western portion is closed by
two straight lines, which form an obtuse angle projecting
inland. Some names are on the continent and are difficult to
decipher. Cuba and "Spagnola" are misplaced and somewhat out of proportion.

There are still preserved, in various parts of the world,
three globes and the gores of a fourth from the early part
of the sixteenth century, which Messrs. Stevens and Coote
believe to be all from the same hand, namely that of Johann
Schoener, "the most distinguished professor of mathematics
and geography then in Germany." The oldest of these is
probably that known as the Hunt-Lenox globe, in the Lenox
Library of New York, and possibly made as early as 1505 or
1507. It is of copper, about 4½ inches in diameter, and represents America as a number of islands. The next one in
point of age is known as the Frankfort globe, because preserved in that city, and dates probably from about the year
1515. The third and most important one is preserved in
Nuremberg, and dates from the year 1520. On this is represented far to the north " Terra Corterealis," near which is the
inscription " Anno Christi 1501." Here again we find the
name Cuba applied to what appears to be the mainland of
America, which extends from near the equator to 55 or 60
degrees north. It also bears the name "Parias," one of the
names connected with South America ever since the days of
Columbus, and which is in fact repeated in South America on
this globe. Notwithstanding this fact it is difficult to believe

that the existence of Florida was not known in the year 1520, especially to a man of Schoener's knowledge. The fourth globe, or rather set of gores, ascribed to the same hand, is referred to the year 1523, and a copy of it is published with the others, in Coote's edition of Stevens on Schoener. It is very simple, and contains but few names. However, that of Florida is especially worthy of notice, as this is perhaps the oldest drawing on which it appears.

Though, as we have seen, there were Frenchmen in the New World in the very beginning of the century, the first official expedition which that government sent to America was in 1524. This was placed under the command of Giovanni Verrazano, a Florentine by birth, who, at an early age, entered the service of King Francis I. of France, and became a most successful corsair against the Spanish. He first touched the western continent at about 34 degrees north latitude, perhaps at Cape Fear. Thence he sailed 50 leagues toward the south, and then directing his vessel northward, he explored the coasts for three months, reaching probably to Newfoundland. The journal of the voyage which remains to us " mentions only one date and names but one locality,"— which facts account for our vague knowledge of the results of the expedition. "It is probable," says H. H. Bancroft, "that a large part of the United States coast was for the first time explored during this voyage, which also completed the discovery of the whole eastern shore-line of America, except probably a short but indefinite distance in South Carolina and Georgia, between the limits reached by Ponce de Leon in 1513 and by Verrazano; one intermediate point having also been visited by Aillon in 1520."

In the two succeeding years, Spaniards were on the coast of the present United States; 1525 witnessing the only expedition which they ever sent to the far north, that of Estévan Gomez, who explored the eastern coasts of America from Newfoundland to an unknown distance south, at any rate below New York, and possibly to Georgia or Florida. The next year came Aillon, who first touched at South Carolina, at the mouth of a river which he called the Jordan, and sailed thence some distance northward "at least to Cape Fear, and probably much farther."

In the grand-ducal library of Weimar there is a large map on parchment, made in the year 1527, by an anonymous cosmographer of the Spanish king, at Seville. It is seven feet, two inches long, and two feet, ten inches wide, and represents the then known world. It is framed and under glass, and is justly considered one of the great treasures of the library. Just how it came there, is not known; but Kohl, who has published a facsimile of the American part, supposes that it was carried to Germany by the Emperor Charles V., as an official map of reference, during one of his voyages from Spain. As to the name of the cosmographer who made it, opinions differ; Kohl inclining to the belief that it is the work of Ferdinand Columbus, son of the admiral, while Harrisse ascribes it to Nuña Garcia de Toreno, and Coote, in editing Stevens on Schoener, thinks it the work of Ribero, and a precursor of his map of 1529, which is also in the same room at Weimar. A careful comparison of the two, it seems to us, can scarcely fail to convince the unprejudiced mind that the latter supposition is the most natural. The points of similarity are so great in non-essentials, such as the astrolabe, the quadrant, the scrolls containing names, etc., the very matters wherein the copier of another man's geographical work would be most likely to desire to show originality; while there is no slavish copying of names, wherein the latter work is much more full and explicit, indicating that the two years intervening between the making of the maps had been spent in gathering new information, which was applied without any reference to a show of slavish consistency with the former work; while at the same time, favorite fancies of ornament were apparently retained unconsciously.

The maps are drawn in plane projection, with compass lines, and also with the equator, tropics, and polar circles.

Perhaps the most noticeable feature, after the beauty of the work, is the absence of imaginary lands, which are so prominent on most of the maps of that age. The principal meridian is drawn through the Cape Verde Islands, from which was to be measured the distance to the line of demarcation between the possessions of Spain and Portugal; and that line, marked by the flags of the two countries on either side, is placed according to the Spanish interpretation of the treaty of Tordesillas, by which the two governments had sought to settle their differences in reference to the matter.

This line passes through "Tierra de los Bretones," lying between 45 and 50 degrees of north latitude; it crosses the northern coast-line of South America at the equator, somewhat west of the mouth of a large river bearing the name "Marahom," meant for Marañon, an old name for the Amazon; and it continues through the continent to the mouth of the "R. Jordan," now the La Plata, in 35 degrees south. This Portuguese part of South America receives its present name of "El Brasil." The map gives an almost unbroken coast-line from 62 degrees north to 54 degrees south, abandoning the old idea of a strait somewhere between these two points; and instead, represents the Strait of Magellan, the existence of which had now been known in Spain for five years. The northern extremity of the map is occupied by a territory designated as "Tiera del Labrador," a name which is probably the only remnant of Portuguese exploration in North America. The coast is drawn in an east and west line, lying between 55° and 60° of latitude, containing no other names, and separated by a narrow strait from the coast lying to the west. The latter is called "Los Bacallaos," and is provided with 14 names, none of which, to my knowledge, are now in use. To the south-west of this region is the "Tierra de los Bretones," already mentioned, on which there are two local names. Here a large river, flowing from the north empties its waters into a prominent bay; this may be the Penobscot, but it is

2

practically impossible to determine positively which river is thereby meant. Between this and " La Florida," there are 11 local names, to which are added 4 on the west side of the latter. Then follow 16 names which are of no special interest to us; but the 17th is the designation of a river flowing into a prominent bay, which is generally taken to mean the Mississippi, and here receives the name " R. del spiritu sancto." Keeping on to the southwest, we find the 15th name, " R. Panuco," one of the earliest names on the continent of North America which is still in use. Then follow 21 more names to the little islands represented between the mainland and " Iveatan," which is also shown as an island. The country southwest of the Gulf of Mexico receives the name adopted by Cortes, when he had conquered it a few years previous, namely " Nova Spaña." It is also worthy of remark that the name " Mexico " is found inland, and is doubtless intended for the city of Mexico, which was however at that time generally called Temixtitlan. The latter is said to be a Spanish corruption of the more usual aboriginal Tenochtitlan, and Mexico was one of its wards or districts. Another derivation is from Mexitli the Aztec war-god (Isaac Taylor, *Words and Places*). Central America has 20 names on the north coast. South America's coast-line is thickly dotted with local names, of which we have already mentioned several. As to the West Indies we would expect to find quite an accurate knowledge displayed, and in this we are not disappointed. Leaving aside the more prominent islands, which are already on earlier maps drawn with tolerable accuracy, we note here " La bermuda ;" also " barbudos," which is probably the Barbuda of to-day. No imaginary antarctic continent is here depicted, as was at that time, and even much later, so customary on maps ; but there is represented only the short coast-line of the strait through which Magellan had passed, south of which is the name he gave to those lands, " tierra del fuegos." To the strait he gave the name " Victoria," after one of his ships; but this map shows that officially his own name had been already conferred on his greatest discovery.[1]

Diego Ribero's map of 1529 is of almost exactly the same size as that of 1527, and the comparison of the two affords a good object lesson in historical geography. Especially striking is this in the case of Peru, the coast of which had been explored by Pizarro in 1525–27, but news of which must have reached Spain too late to be incorporated in the map of 1527. The later map is also richly provided with historical remarks, manifesting a desire on the part of the cartographer to embody in his work all the information possible. In outline the Atlantic coast on both maps is almost identical; but much more knowledge of detail is embodied in the later one. This is marked on the eastern coast of the present United States, where the results of the voyages of Ayllon and Gomez find place on the later map. While there are but fourteen names between Florida and Bacallaos on the map of 1527, that of 1529 contains more than thirty in the same space, besides several historical remarks. On the latter are also embodied the results of the ill-fated voyage of Sebastian Cabot in 1526, by which the waters of the river Plata and its chief tributaries were first made known to Europeans. Mexico is well drawn, and gives the results of Cortes' conquest, including the Villa Rica de la Vera Cruz, which he founded, and which, after two removes, may be considered the beginning of the modern city of Vera Cruz. "Ivcatan" is better shaped than before, but still continues to be represented as an island. Cuba is represented as extending through twelve degrees of longitude and four of latitude, a nearer approach to its real extent than was usual in those days. On this map, we see for the first time, I believe, the name "Haiti" applied to Espagnola; and "S. Domingo" is its principal settlement. In fact there are on this map quite a number of names with familiar aspect.

---

[1] Mr. Hale in Winsor's *Nar. and Crit. Hist.* (II, 604), says that the name of Eleven Thousand Virgins was given to the strait by Magellan.

Here are Cape San Antonio and Cape Cruz in Cuba; Peru for the first time; also "Guatimala," and the rivers Parana, Uruay, evidently the present Uruguay, and Paraguay; here is also "Tiera de Papagones," the land of the Patagonians or big-footed giants, about the existence of whom there has been so much controversy. The name "Tierra de los Fuegos" reminds us of the fires that Magellan saw there when entering the strait, whose discovery and the consequent first circumnavigation of the earth have made his name famous; and the little settlements of Darien, Panama, and Cartagena call attention to the fact that the maps of the new world were some day to wear a political aspect. The rivers Panuco and San Francisco, the islands of Cozumel and Trinidad, the capes Catoche and St. Augustine, are so familiar to us that, on this map, we begin to feel at home.

Such maps as these two treasures of the Weimar library go very far toward raising our respect for the cosmographers of the sixteenth century. The American part of them has been published in fac-simile, together with a long dissertation, by Dr. Kohl, which can be found in a number of our libraries. Rough sketches of these and other maps, such as have been published in great numbers during recent years, give one no adequate idea of the originals. These sketches are indeed useful to the seeker after historical knowledge; and we are greatly indebted to the historians whose works are so richly illustrated with them; if, however, our national government had a just idea of the dignity and usefulness of history, it would make generous provision for the publication of fac-similes of all the leading maps bearing on our history; and could thereby make a fitting tribute to the celebration of the four hundredth anniversary of the discovery of America.

Already at the end of the third decade of the sixteenth century we find the Spanish government, at least, in possession of knowledge in quite an accurate degree, of the north and east coasts of South America, of the Gulf of Mexico, and the West India Islands, together with a less accurate acquaintance with the Atlantic coast of the United States and further north. But the Spanish government kept this knowledge so far as possible within its own realms; and other nations did much to bring a knowledge of those regions into the consciousness of Europe at large. In noticing later maps, we shall leave aside then what they contain as to the parts already accurately represented, and confine our attention to the furtherance of knowledge of those coasts, which, up to the period where we now leave off, were not at all or only inaccurately known in Europe.

II.

Development of Pacific-Coast Geography.

A general idea of the discovery of the Pacific seems to be, that Balboa and his companions took a promenade one day to the top of a hill in the vicinity of their settlement, whence they descried with wonder the broad expanse of that mighty ocean; then with boyish glee, ran down the slope, dashed into the water, and with a flourish, took possession of it in the name of their sovereign. How different from the reality! Selecting carefully 190 of the hardiest men in the little settlement of Antigua, in the northwest corner of South America, Vasco Nuñez de Balboa sailed four days toward the northwest, and landed near the village of a friendly chief. He had with him also, 1000 Indians as warriors and carriers, and a pack of bloodhounds which were to aid in the work of subduing the natives. The point at which he now found himself was not the site of Aspinwall, whence one at present departs for the short and easy ride through the magnificent tropical forest, that delights the eye without impeding the progress of the traveller. Balboa was at some distance to the southeast of this, just opposite the bay of San Miguel. Before him lay an unbroken forest, rendered almost impenetrable by tangled undergrowth, and beset with tribes of warlike and hostile natives. It cost him one battle, and many days of hard marching, to reach the summit of the mountain range whence, his Indian guides told him, could be seen the broad expanse of another ocean. The most elevated point was a bare rock, below which a halt was ordered, and "Vasco Nuñez advanced
22

alone. His should be the first European eye to behold what there was to behold, and that without peradventure. With throbbing heart he mounted the topmost eminence which crowned these sea-dividing hills. Then, as in the lifting of a veil, a scene of primeval splendor burst on his enraptured gaze, such as might fill with joy an archangel sent to explore a new creation. There it lay, that boundless unknown sea, spread out before him, far as the eye could reach, in calm majestic beauty, glittering like liquid crystal in the morning sun. . . . Dropping on his knees, he poured forth praises and thanksgiving to the author of that glorious creation for the honor of its discovery. The soldiers then pressed forward, gazed enchanted likewise, and likewise assumed the attitude of prayer : for however ungodly were their lives, these cavaliers were always fond of praying." Years before this, Columbus had been told of the existence of a large body of water on the other side of the mountains seen from the coast of the Gulf of Mexico; he was, however, convinced that this whole region was but a part of Asia, and that accordingly such a body of water could be only the Bay of Bengal. Balboa brought back to Antigua gold to the value of over 40,000 *pesos*, or dollars of the time, together with an immense store of pearls, not to speak of cotton cloth, native weapons, and 800 Indian slaves. Furthermore he had subdued all the nations through whose territories he had passed, gained the most of them to friendship, and all this without the loss of a man. The loadstone had been found which could draw the Spaniards to all the perils of discovery and conquest; so this region, and the still richer fields to which it opened the way, were marked for future conquest.

From this time forth the excursions of the Spaniards to the Pacific coast were numerous ; but with the characteristic secrecy of the time, they did not publish the results thereof to the world at large. Some idea of it, however, gradually made its way throughout Europe, and we soon find it assuming shape on the cartographical representations. The Frankfort globe of 1515, the Nuremberg one of 1520, and the Apianus map of the same date, all bear testimony to the fact. The real knowledge of the Pacific ocean and its American coast was very scant, and the cartographers did not possess even all that the navigators and the Spanish government did. Accordingly the maps of that early time give us but the crudest idea of this part of the New World.

We shall find, nevertheless, that for some time to come many Europeans believed that North America was a part of the great eastern stretch of Asia; but from the third decade of the sixteenth century it was established that at least South America was separate therefrom, or at least only connected with it perhaps by a long strait. In the year 1520, Magellan passed through the strait that now bears his name, and called the great body of water into which he thence issued " Mare Pacificum." However, this discovery was not positively known in Spain till two years afterward, when his ship returned to Spain via the Cape of Good Hope; though it had been thought probable, from the report of some who had accompanied Magellan into the strait, and had then abandoned him in order to hurry back with the news of an enterprise but half accomplished. But the Pacific coast of America was to be explored mainly from the centre to the north and south, not from either end toward the centre. The extension of geographical knowledge must precede the cartographical representation of that knowledge; unless indeed we busy ourselves with the fancies of men who were more anxious to attract the public than to aid in the spread of scientific learning. Mr. H. H. Bancroft has an interesting chapter on this very theme, but it lies outside our purpose to deal with it. There had already been exploring parties sent out from the isthmus in the years 1514, 1515 and 1519, before Cortes conquered Mexico; but from the time that he was in possession of that country, there was manifest a determination to know the Pacific coast of the land more accurately, and preparations on a large scale were made to explore that coast, especially toward the north. Before the year 1522, Cortes had discovered three points on the coast from Tehuantepec to Zacatula; and this same year there was an expedition sent out from the isthmus, of which one portion under Gonzalez Davila, went by land to Nicaragua, while the other, coasting northward, may have gone as far as Tehuantepec, if the recorded distances are to be believed. Ten years later, Hurtado de Mendoza reached the coast of Sinaloa, opposite the southern extremity of Lower California; and was followed the succeeding year (1533) by Jiminez, who touched the southern point of the peninsula of California, and supposed the whole to be an island. In 1539 Ulloa reached the head waters of the Gulf of California, examining more or less closely both the east and west sides, thus proving the peninsular form of Lower California; he touched its southernmost point, and sailed up its western coast to the vicinity of Cedros Island, in twenty-nine degrees north.

The earliest accurate representation of any part of the Pacific coast that we have, is that on the anonymous Spanish map of 1527, on which there is given the result of the discoveries at least as late as those of 1522; for at the most northerly point is mentioned *Sierra de gil Goncalez Dauila*, evidently named from the chief of the exploring party of that year, of which we have already spoken. The southern discoveries appear to have been unknown to the author of the map, as there is nothing given south of the Gulf of San Miguel. The town of Panama, which had been founded in 1519, also finds place. This name was probably abbreviated from that of Tubanamá, who, says H. H. Bancroft, "was reputed the richest as well as the strongest chieftain of these mountains, and was the terror of the neighboring nations." In all there are 35 names on the part of the Pacific coast here drawn, and there are also two names inland, of which it is difficult to say whether they are intended to designate places inland or on the coast. This same year, Robert Thorne, residing at Seville, Spain, sent to England his map of the world, on which the southern coast of Central America is drawn, but he seems to have possessed no accurate knowledge of its details.

On the following map, that of Ribero, of 1529, the Pacific coast-line extends southward to about the tenth degree of south latitude, where we find the name, "chinchax." The whole region is called 'Perv;' thus showing the acquaintance of the author with the expedition of Pascual de Andogoya, who in 1522 sailed from Panama to a point six or seven days' journey south of the Gulf of San Miguel, to the province under the command of a chief named Birú. It was principally on account of the information gained on this expedition that Pizarro was later led to undertake the conquest of the rich countries on the west coast of South America; although as early as the first exploration of Balboa, news of the existence of great wealth south of the isthmus had been obtained; and Pizarro, it is worthy of remark, was one of Balboa's companions on that occasion. The marvellous accounts of the riches of Peru, which were substantiated by the great quantities of gold and pearls sent thence to the mother country, excited widespread curiosity; and adventurers in vast numbers thronged there. Fortunately for history, there came also some with a literary turn, who have left us valuable descriptions of what they there saw and learned. Pizarro had secured from the Spanish crown the right of conquest over a stretch of two hundred leagues along the coast; and the right of conquest of the country further south was ceded to another adventurer, by name Almagro. These two, at first friends and partners in the project, later became the most bitter enemies; which fact, however, was probably to the advantage of a rapid progress in the knowledge of the more southerly parts; for it compelled Almagro to seek his prize in the less attractive and poorer south. So within a very few years after the first discovery, the coast became known with a certain degree of accuracy, as far south as the site of Valparaiso; while the interior was fast being opened up to the conquerors. In 1540 Alonzo de Camargo passed through the Straits of Magellan, touched the coast of Chili at latitude 38 degrees 30 minutes south, and sailed on to Arequipa in Peru; thus, so

far as known, completing for the first time the knowledge of
the outline of the South American coast. The knowledge thus
gained by Camargo was by no means perfect, if we are to judge
it by the maps of Ortelius and others, that represent the coast
of Chili projecting quite as far to the west as does Peru. This
however, should occasion no surprise on our part, when we
consider that these navigators were not employed in making
an accurate survey of the coast, but in the universal hunt for
gold. Moreover they had not the instruments to make
accurate observations, if they had cared to do so. When we
call to mind that this was in the days of Copernicus, to whom
was due "the overthrow of the Ptolemaic system and the total
renovation of the science of astronomy;" and when we think
of the crudity of instruments and methods of even the foremost
astronomers of this time, should we wonder that simple,
practical pilots did not produce better results? The wonder
is rather that many of them did so well under such adverse
circumstances. On the Nancy globe of about 1550, the
Pacific coast-line of South America is in general quite accurately drawn; and here we may leave the subject. Though
a number of the later maps still retain the old inaccuracies,
a fairly exact knowledge of the western coast of South
America had already been gained, not only by Spanish
explorers and their fellow countrymen, but also beyond that
country, to such an extent that we may be justified in asserting,
that from the middle of the sixteenth century, a fair knowledge
of the Pacific coast of South America had penetrated into the
mind of educated Europe.

We now come to a consideration of the geographical development of the knowledge of the coast of California and the
north-western part of North America. Rumors of great
quantities of gold to be found in this direction also, caused
the Spaniards, for a series of years, to make voyages hither
from their newly conquered country of Mexico; but as
Nature here kept her secret most cunningly from them, they
gradually relinquished the search, did comparatively little to

foster the settlements already begun there, yielded their claims in part, first to the English, then to the United States; and were finally compelled by war to relinquish all to their now more powerful neighbor. Then, as if by magic, the door of Nature's treasure-house was opened, and all the world gazed in wonder at the uncounted wealth poured out therefrom. Still further to the north, a country of fine harbors and magnificent scenery was gradually brought to a knowledge of the Europeans; but for a long period this region also was considered of but little value. Time, however, has shown that sea and earth there are abundantly stored with riches, and it requires only hardihood and energy to bring them to light.

Let us now follow somewhat in detail the growth of this knowledge. The western coast of North America is in many respects a striking contrast to the eastern. The mountains are nearer the ocean and the coast-line is much less broken by bays, inlets, and the mouths of large rivers. On this account the early navigators were compelled to proceed warily, as the good harbors were but few, and these far distant from each other. Moreover, the experience of a majority of the early mariners on this part of the Pacific Ocean was such, that they would never have conferred upon it the name given by Magellan to its southern portion; and it was only by slow degrees that the entire body of water between America and Asia came to be known by the name Pacific. The history of the exploration of the western coast of the United States and British America is a story of peril by storm and fog, in worm-eaten ships, without proper supplies of food and water, and in general of untold misery and death caused by privation and exposure.

How much is due to Spanish exploration of the coast of California can be summarized in brief. The first three decades of the sixteenth century had passed without their getting much if any to the north of the present southern boundary of the United States. The most important expedition which they sent out in this direction during the century was that of 1542,

under Cabrillo, which in spite of fogs, storms and adverse
winds, slowly made its way along the coast toward the north,
giving names and making observations, till they thought they
had reached the latitude of the 44th parallel.   Mr. H. H. Bancroft, who has made a careful analysis of the records of the
voyage, is of the opinion that Cabrillo himself reached no
higher than 42 degrees.   But he died, and the explorations
were continued under his successor in command, Ferrelo;
and he may possibly have proceeded as far north as the 43d
parallel.   Neither of them landed however north of Point
Conception, in latitude 34° 26′.   During the whole of the
remainder of the sixteenth century the Spaniards did not
improve on the knowledge of these parts gained by this
expedition.

Though the Spanish government was doubtless promptly in
receipt of information as to the results of this voyage, that
knowledge failed for a long time to penetrate to the makers of
maps.   The Nancy globe, already mentioned, has not a hint
of the existence of an ocean west of the present United States,
but represents Mexico as a southeasterly projection of Asia.
To the west of Mexico, here spelled Messico, is placed " Asia
Magna," and north of it, " Asia Orientalis ;" while the Gulf
of Mexico is hardly recognizable under the appellation "Mare
Cathayum," the name then generally given to the Chinese
Sea.   This supposed connection between the mainland of Asia
and the New World must never be lost sight of in studying
the geography of the period ; for it is the key to much that
would otherwise be absolutely nonsensical on the part of cosmographers of the time.

There was also another element of fancy that played an
important part in the geography of this period.   The desire
to find a northern passage to the riches of India and Japan
had been expressed as early as the period of the Cabots.   After
the discovery of the southern strait by Magellan, there was a
fixed determination, especially on the part of England and
France, to find a corresponding passage in the north.   What

men earnestly long for, they frequently come to believe true
and practicable; which characteristic of human nature resulted
in this case in the appearance of actual descriptions, nay even
pictures, of a northerly strait connecting the Atlantic and
Pacific, which no one had ever seen or passed through. Spanish
discoveries produced the separation, on the maps, of the
southern part of North America from the mainland of Asia.
But it was the belief in the imaginary Straits of Anian that
first brought upon the maps a representation of North America
as a great continent absolutely separate from the Orient.
Many maps of the period serve to illustrate what has just
been said. The earliest representation of this known to me
is the Schoener globe of 1523, where a broad open strait in the
far north connects the Atlantic and Pacific oceans. Perhaps
the best known of them all was that of Ortelius, published in
1570 in his great work entitled "Theatrum Orbis Terrarum."
On his map of the world, an unbroken coast-line extends from
the Straits of Magellan in 52 degrees south to "Anian,"
which is placed between 60 and 65 degrees north latitude.
As this was one of the maps in the first of modern atlases,
and its author enjoyed the reputation of being, after Mercator,
the greatest geographer of the age, we may well understand
how the work became popular, and went through five revised
editions during the author's life time, and became the common
foundation for many geographies compiled by later writers.

In 1579, Francis Drake, on his famous voyage round the
world, landed on the western coast of North America, probably at about 43 degrees north latitude. Thence he coasted
toward the south until he found a convenient harbor where he
could beach his ship. Here he remained a month; and while
the ship was being repaired, some little inland exploring was
also done. The point where he first landed and the harbor
where he passed a month are both subjects of sharp controversy. The errors in astronomical reckoning, common at
that period, have been already touched upon. Nor is it easy
to fix, by the meagre description left us, the locality visited.

Accuracy of observation and statement is rarely found, except where men are trained to it, and a description of only the general characteristics of a harbor might answer for any one of several ports. That Drake's halting place was the present Bay of San Francisco seems to us highly improbable, for two reasons: 1, that a month's sojourn in such a magnificent harbor, on a coast where even passably good harbors are rare, would have called forth such exclamations of unusual surprise and pleasure on the part of the chronicler of the expedition as we do not find; and 2, that it is not more probable that Drake found the Golden Gate than other navigators who had passed and repassed along that coast, without ever suspecting the existence thereof. Just outside the entrance to the Bay of San Francisco are several islets that, to a navigator feeling his way along an unknown coast, would rather lead him to steer for the open sea than attract him to search behind them for a magnificent harbor which lies not only behind those islands, but in truth so encircled by the long arms of the mainland that, from the sea, there appears to be not even promise of a safe shelter. And the fact remains, that the bay remained unknown, at least to the Spaniards, until discovered in 1769 by accident, from the land side. Drake called the region along whose coast he had sailed, New Albion; and this name long continued to appear on maps of this part of America; while England afterwards laid claim to the whole of this part of the continent on the strength of Drake's discoveries.

Ten years after Drake's voyage a well known map of the world was published by Hakluyt, the greatest collector of his day of information as to everything relating to voyages of discovery. On this map we see America represented as entirely distinct from Asia, although their separation was not proven till the famous voyage of Behring, nearly 140 years later. But the imaginary Strait of Anian is there, that much dreamed-of passage in the north from the Atlantic to the Pacific. On the mainland, at about 60 degrees north, there appears the name " Anian regnum," Kingdom of Anian, which is bounded by the aforesaid imaginary strait. This body of water tends first toward the northeast till it reaches between 70 and 80 degrees of north latitude, and then runs due east till it connects with the Atlantic Ocean. But the whole region north of 40 degrees, as depicted, is manifestly imaginary, and from its appearance, convinces the beholder that the compiler knew nothing of that which he was attempting to represent.

At the beginning of the seventeenth century, the Spanish government sent out another, and practically a last expedition to make discoveries on the western coast of the present United States. It was under the command of Vizcaino, and so far as we know, went but little if any further north than Cabrillo and Ferrelo had done more than half a century antecedent. However, a map was made showing the results of the voyage, which map displays a more exact acquaintance with the coast than any previous one had done; and this map was not improved upon for a century and a half following. Already we find a number of local names that have since remained permanent. There are Cape Mendocino, and Cape San Lucas; also the names Monterey and San Diego, here applied also to capes, and to-day the names of cities in their respective vicinities. The island of Santa Barbara also had been already given the name that it still bears. But such expeditions were expensive both in life and treasure; and as they did not bring in the desired return of gold, the Spanish government could not be induced to continue them. The Indians had learned by this time to play upon the imagination of the Spaniards; and wherever the latter came, asking for information as to where gold was to be found, they heard a story of marvelous riches still further to the north. But as the place of immense riches ever receded like the will-o'-the-wisp, from the path of the Spaniards, they became weary in the pursuit, and gradually relinquished it. From now on, their chief thought as to the north was, lest another nation should find a northwest passage to the Pacific.

There was a long cessation of explorations in this vicinity during the seventeenth century; but nevertheless geographical works continued to be published, as did also descriptions of travels, illustrated with maps; and for all of these works maps were made, their authors but too often supplying from their imagination what they lacked in actual knowledge. During this period was spread abroad the fable that California was an island. As early as 1539, the Spaniards had already, as we have seen, explored the Gulf of California to its head waters, and had satisfied themselves of the peninsular character of the body of land lying to the west. The original source of the error in representing it as an island, is not disclosed to us; but so far as known the first such representation of it is that on the map which Purchas published in his celebrated book called the Pilgrims, in the year 1625. The island extends from Cape S. Lucas in 23 degrees north to Cape Blanco in 42 degrees north. The general trend of the Pacific coast between these points is well drawn; but inland there runs an imaginary strait almost due north from the Gulf of California to about the 42d parallel, and there it empties into a bay formed like the Bay of Biscay, in a great right angle. The error thus given to the world long continued to deceive the public as to the true geography of the region.[1] Although the results of Drake's voyage must then have been well known in England, there is nothing on this map which would lead us to suspect that its maker had any knowledge of the great bay which is to-day the pride of Californians.

---

[1] An inscription in the S. W. corner of the map reads as follows: "California sometymes supposed to be a part of y* westerne continent, but scince by a Spanish charte taken by y* Hollanders it is found to be a goodly Islande; the length of the west shoare beeing about 500 leagues from Cape Mendocino to the South Cape thereof called Cape St. Lucas; as appeareth both by that Spanish chart and by the relation of Francis Gaule whereas in the ordinarie Charts it is sett downe to be 1700 leagues." Worthy of remark is the fact that another map in the same volume gives quite a satisfactory. representation of the Gulf and Peninsula of California.

3

Early Spanish and English navigators had failed to explore the western coast of America further north than the 43d or 44th parallel of latitude. There remained yet a vast unknown northwest, about which speculation was rife; but which hardly promised to pay for the trouble of its exploration. As far as any knowledge to the contrary went, North America was still a mere projection or elongation of Asia; though it was devoutly hoped and suspected that the contrary was true. The absolute knowledge of the fact was to be revealed by a man of a nationality which up to that time had not taken part in exploring the New World, and who was in the service of a nation that was looked upon by its neighbors as little better than barbarous. Among the many new ventures undertaken in the reign of Peter the Great of Russia, one of the prominent ones was that of the exploration and settlement of Siberia. During his life various parties had been organized and sent out for this purpose; and the same policy was continued after his death. In order to carry out his great improvements in Russian life, manufactures, etc., Peter the Great had found it necessary to import into his realm many foreigners, in great part Germans. Among these latter came one named Vitus Bering, or Behring, a man of almost forbidding aspect, but energetic and capable, at least in his earlier undertakings. Being both foreign and repellent in manner, he succeeded in making himself cordially hated by his Russian subordinates. Yet it is to this man that we owe the first demonstration of the fact that Russia and America are indeed separate continents. Having crossed the great wastes of Siberia, he built a ship on the eastern coast; and in the summer of 1728 he passed East Cape, the most easterly point of Asia, whence the land turns abruptly toward the west. Although from this point the coast of America is but 36 miles distant, nothing of the western continent was seen on this voyage, by Behring and his men. However, at this we should not be surprised, as the region is one where fogs prevail for a considerable portion of the year. Two years later, we are told, "Krupiscef and Gwozdef, following Behring, actually came in sight of the American continent, along which they coasted southward for two days" (H. H. Bancroft). However, nothing definite seems to be known as to the exact region thus visited. After their first essay, Behring and his men spent several years in preparations and quarrelling, and in 1741 they started out again on the waters of the northern Pacific, determined this time to find America. They had two ships, the second one being in command of a Russian named Chirikof. On the voyage Behring seems to have displayed such a spirit of weak vacillation that one is tempted to think him in his dotage. The two vessels became separated, and that under Chirikof was the first to sight land, probably near the present Sitka. Somewhat later Behring came in sight of Mount St. Elias, from which point he sailed first west and then southwest, and discovered the Shumagin Islands, south of the western extremity of the Alaskan peninsula, to which islands he gave their present name. Steering thence for Siberia, he was wrecked on a little island that still bears his name. There he succumbed to the hardships and privations that had filled so large a portion of his life. Some of his companions, however, managed to eke out an existence through the winter. Among other booty, they succeeded in killing some seals, whose furs they took back with them to Siberia, when finally rescued. Thus the seal may be said to have been discovered; and to that discovery is due the fact, that henceforth this region has attracted an ever increasing number of daring sailors to its shores. As a result of these discoveries, the Academy of Sciences of St. Petersburg, published in 1758 a map of Alaska, with the names in the French language. It shows various points from Behring strait south, to what it designates as the "Port of Francis Drake, falsely called the Port of St. Francis." The portions of the coast-line still unknown are marked by dotted lines, which connect in a conventional manner the heavy lines of the known coast. The routes of Behring and Chirikof are also laid down.

During the same year that saw the completion of the discovery of the northeast coast of Asia by Behring, there was born, of humble parentage, in England, James Cook, who was destined to become one of the greatest navigators of the age. Into his early career we have no time to enter. His last work was to seek from the Pacific side the long wished-for northern passage to the Atlantic. Leaving the Sandwich Islands, which he had discovered, he sailed toward America in the summer of 1778, and first sighted the mainland near the 43d parallel. Thence he followed the coast toward the north, approaching it at various points. He entered Nootka Sound, and adopted for it the aboriginal name, which still appears on our maps. Far to the north he entered, with high hope of succeeding in his mission, a promising inlet. However, his progress was soon blocked by land, and he returned to the open ocean. The inlet retains to-day the name of its hardy discoverer. Nothing daunted, he pushed on farther toward the north, examining islands and mainland, ever hoping and ever doomed to renewed disappointment, till at last his progress was arrested by impenetrable ice. The neighboring cape he named Icy Point; whence, forced to abandon his project, he turned again toward the sunny south. He made a map of the coast, embodying the results, not only of his own observations, but also all that he could learn of the Russian explorations. With this voyage, the discovery of the western coast of America may be said to have been completed, at least in outline, though a vast deal remained for navigators to explore regarding the details thereof. And here we leave the subject.

This sketch of the historical development of the coast lines of America in the consciousness of Europe would not be complete without some notice of the representations of an imaginary Antarctic continent south of the Straits of Magellan, and the substitution therefor of the complex of islands now known to exist there. On Magellan's first entrance into the strait, fires were seen along the coast, whence he gave it the name it has ever since borne, Terra del Fuego, or Land of Fire. From the days of Ptolemy, it was a matter of tradition that the Indian Ocean, like the Mediterranean, was an inland sea; and that consequently there must exist to the south of it another, as yet unknown continent. Long before Magellan's discovery, there appeared on Behaim's globe a strait represented very nearly in the position of the one found by that explorer; and south of it there was drawn a great continent. The representations of this mythic body of land are larger or smaller, according to the liveliness of imagination of their respective authors. On some maps there is drawn a continent with its centre at the south pole, and extending thence to an enormous distance in all directions. On others it is much smaller, but still of great extent; while the famous maps of 1527 and 1529 already referred to several times, give us but the small extent of coast-line, which had been actually seen by the navigators, and leaves the rest out, to be supplied from later explorations. In 1578 Francis Drake passed through the straits on his voyage round the world, and then sailed to the southwest until he sighted the end of this group of islands, and convinced himself that there was no continent there. In 1616 two Dutch navigators named Lemaire and Schouten passed south of the group from the Atlantic to the Pacific, and christened the southern extremity Cape Hoorn, after the latter's native place, a small town on the shores of the Zuyder Zee. Thus the extent of this group of islands became known. However, the non-existence of an Antarctic continent was not proven until Captain Cook made his famous explorations in the south seas, discovering and naming numbers of groups of islands, but finding no trace of the enormous continent that geographers had represented as existing there. Thus actual knowledge took the place of ignorance, and the Untrue was shamed away when exposed to the searching light of day.

III.

Geography of the Interior and Polar Regions.

After Columbus had once shown the way across the Atlantic, it was a comparatively easy matter to follow in his wake, and extend the voyage somewhat further along the coast than he had done; likewise, after Magellan had penetrated the mysteries of the straits that now bear his name, the discovery of the Pacific coasts was made possible in ships sailing from Europe. But the exploration of the interior of the country, traversed by unbridged streams and lofty mountain ranges, and largely filled with almost impenetrable forests, was an entirely different matter. We have seen in the preceding lecture how many difficulties and dangers accompanied the short route of Balboa across the Isthmus of Panama ; yet that was but a bagatelle to what must be undergone before the whole vast continent could be opened to and subjugated by the European and his descendants.

The work here was not only more difficult in itself, but it lacked also the strong motive, especially in North America, which attracted the earliest navigators, namely, the presence of the precious metals. Very possibly, it is owing to this fact, that the entire North American continent is not, like the South American, now in the hands of the Latin races ; for the Spaniards made numerous attempts to explore and settle the north, so long as there seemed to be a possibility of finding gold there ; and only retired from the struggle when convinced of its non-existence. Otherwise the struggle for the possession of the northern part of our continent would have been a three-fold one; and who can tell what would have been its issue?

Another fact must also be borne in mind, and that is the then backward state of mathematical geography. Errors of five degrees of latitude have already been noticed ; but in longitude the uncertainty was even greater, navigators misreckoning therein even to the extent of twenty degrees. Consequently, even after the Pacific coast was to a certain extent known, no one could tell the exact relation between it and the Atlantic, or could calculate the immense stretch of country that lies between the two. The great river basins of the Amazon and La Plata offered unusual facilities for penetrating to the interior of the southern continent, while the silver of the one region, and the famous hard woods of the other, lent the necessary stimulus to their exploration ; and on the Pacific coast, the wealth of Peru was an attraction which would have induced the Spaniards to go through fire and water, if necessary, to obtain it. The same is true of Mexico, where the natives had already reached a considerable degree of civilization, and where accordingly provisions during the march of the invader were more easily obtainable; the country was comparatively narrow from coast to coast, and great wealth was there ready collected for the first brave adventurer who, with the products of European skill, should contend against the arms of native manufacture. But, in the territory now occupied by the United States, which in reality is marvelously rich in the precious metals, the early seekers after gold were not successful in finding it, and eventually abandoned the search. For this reason, much of the 3,000,000 square miles which form our territory was allowed to remain in its pristine state until a comparatively late period, when the discovery of vast quantities of gold and silver acted with its old-time attractiveness, and thousands rushed thither to seek their fortunes. Even Canada and a great part of British North America were known long before our western territory, because man had first discovered there wealth-producing articles.

The cartographical productions of the sixteenth and seventeenth centuries have a rather strange appearance to eyes acquainted only with recent maps.

Take, for example, the map of Juan de la Cosa, who necessarily knew nothing of the interior of America. He filled it up with lakes and rivers *ad libitum*, connecting all rivers with lakes, but not all with the sea. Furthermore he gives names on the coast to rivers, as in the case of Rio Negro, but draws nothing to indicate the presence of flowing water there. The same holds good of the early maps generally, until the conquest of Mexico gave cartographers something outside of their imaginations as a foundation for what they depicted beyond the coast-lines. The power of imagination varied with the individual; but practically all have more or less of the fantastic, if we except such unusual productions as the official Spanish maps of 1527 and 1529. Mountains were often visible from the ships of the explorers, and mouths of rivers were frequently entered for fresh water, or in hopes of finding the traditional passage to the Pacific; thus these two features were the first to attract the attention of the explorers, and consequently were the first features of the interior to appear on the maps; but little, however, was known of the courses of the rivers or of the nature of the mountain ranges. Naturally the interior of Espagnola, and of some of the other islands, was familiar to the Spaniards at an early date; but our attention, in the short time allotted us, must be confined to the mainland. During the conquest of Mexico, Cortes began the founding of cities on the eastern seaboard; and as early as May, 1522, he founded Zacatula on the western coast, a city that still remains in existence. In the meantime, the necessities of the situation had compelled him to send parties of his men in all directions, so that the country was fairly well explored in a short space of time. More or less elaborate accounts of all his doings were sent from time to time to Spain, where he had to defend his reputation from the accusations of his enemies, mainly by showing how much he was doing toward opening up a valuable country for his sovereign. Hither and thither marched his troops, conquering and pillaging; making roads and discovering deposits of the precious metals; ever extending their borders toward both north and south. In Central America, Cortes' men soon arrived at districts already explored by his countrymen coming from the Isthmus of Darien. But toward the north lay a territory of unknown extent, in which Indian tales placed seven cities of untold wealth; and these stories, it was, that lead to the exploration and settlement of New Mexico, at a time when the eastern coast of the present United States possessed not a single European inhabitant. It may as well here be added that the settlement did not thrive, and for a long period, even till toward the close of the eighteenth century, was, in the words of Mr. H. H. Bancroft, "struggling not very zealously, for a bare existence." From 1530 to 1540 various exploring parties traversed this region, reaching perhaps as far north as the fortieth parallel of latitude, and westward into the present territory of Arizona. Several Indian towns were discovered, but they contained very little wealth. However, from this time forth we find on the maps a variety of names, in the interior, sometimes of provinces, sometimes of towns, but generally of uncertain location, as scarcely any two maps agree in this particular.

During the fourth decade of the sixteenth century, Cartier ascended the river St. Lawrence for 500 miles, passing the site of Montreal, and probably reaching the St. Louis Falls. At the end of the same decade, De Soto commenced, in the south, his ill-fated expedition into the interior. As the remnant of De Soto's daring adventurers brought back practically all the information of the interior of the present United States, south of Tennessee and east of the Mississippi, which was gained for a century, it will be worth our while to follow for a moment their supposed route. After a careful study of the records, Mr. H. H. Bancroft is of the opinion that their route was about as follows :—landing at Tampa Bay, they proceeded to near Tallahassee; thence northeast to the Savannah River below Augusta; thence northwest to the line of the present state of Tennessee near Dalton, Georgia; thence southwest to near Mobile Bay, whence they turned toward the northwest and advanced to the famous discovery of the Mississippi, which they first saw not far from the mouth of the Arkansas. Crossing the stream, they penetrated far to the west, without finding that rich kingdom of which they were in search; and returned, deeply disappointed, to the Mississippi, where the leader gave up the ghost, and was secretly buried beneath those waters, the history of which will ever be associated with his name. De Soto was succeeded in command by Luis de Moscoso, under whom the band, greatly reduced in numbers, again turned to the west, marched 150 leagues, till they came in sight of the mountains; then for the last time retraced their course to the Mississippi above the Arkansas, where they, with great difficulty, constructed some frail craft, in which they succeeded in reaching Panuco; and there they found rest among their fellow-countrymen. As the result of this expedition, many names of Indian tribes came to the knowledge of the Spaniards—names which are found, from time to time, on our maps; but with the same result as has been before noticed, namely, that their locality is by no means fixed. During this same fourth decade of the sixteenth century, the conquest of Peru was being vigorously prosecuted; accounts of which brought considerable knowledge of the interior of South America to European cartographers. A little earlier, Sebastian Cabot was making his extended researches into the geography of the basin of the river La Plata, spending five years in the work, and penetrating a thousand miles into the interior; while at the beginning of the fifth decade, Orellana made his descent of the Amazon from the Andes, thus bringing to light the enormous length of that mighty stream. About the middle of the century, Irala, the governor of Buenos Ayres, organized an exploring party which forced a way overland to the Spanish possessions of Peru, and thereby opened communication by land between the Atlantic and Pacific coasts.

Meantime the cartographers came slowly into possession of the knowledge acquired by the discoverers; but their representations gave much less information than the written descriptions. On the Spanish map of 1527, several territorial divisions are named, of which the most important is Nova Spaña; and near this name, we find that of Mexico, but without anything to indicate to what the latter refers. The northeast corner of South America is designated by its present name of El Brasil, while the northwest portion receives the appellation of 'Castila del Oro.' The Amazon under the name of ' Maranhom,' flows from many sources in the southwest. Ribero's map of two years later contains but little that is new, giving the imaginary courses of several rivers, notably the San Francisco of South America. It names the province of Peru, which is lacking on the preceding; and adds several names in North America, from those of explorers, or would-be founders of colonies, but in whose territories there were as yet no Caucasian inhabitants. We note also the name ' Tiera de Patagones,' that given by Magellan to the inhabitants of the southernmost portion of the western continent; and there appears for the first time in Central America the name " Guatimala."

On an Italian map of 1534, the great interior of South America is styled ' Castiglia nuova over Perv,' which recalls the name of the province ceded to Pizarro by the Spanish government, before the conquest of the region, and the adoption by the Spaniards of the native name, or a corruption of the same; for as has been already said, it was also called at an early day Birú. The Spanish name, however, occurs but seldom on maps, the native term from the first taking the lead in popular usance, and the official usage being gradually altered in accordance therewith. On the Oxford map of about 1536, is the name ' rio de la platta,' which I have not noticed on any earlier map, though from this time forth it occurs frequently, and finally becomes general. Thus we see how maps grow, if the term be allowed; for one cartographer not only copies what his predecessors have drawn upon their works, but seeks to add thereto from his own stock of information. Thus it is, that the connection between descriptive and pictorial geography must ever be borne in mind, as both belong to the science, and are equally necessary to its advancement; the one, however, necessarily following the other, in order to show clearly at a glance, the really important matters which might otherwise cost hours of laborious reading to understand. On the map of J. Rotz, of 1542, which gives the names in the English language, the Gulf of St. Lawrence is quite correctly drawn, though the islands in and about it are largely imaginary in their form and number. The whole map indicates that some knowledge of the results of Cartier's voyages had already penetrated to England. On the Medina map of 1549, the "R. de los Amazones" rises in the northwestern part of South America and flows in a southeasterly direction, emptying into the ocean at 5 or 6 degrees south latitude, where it receives the name 'marañon,' thus embodying upon a printed map the results of a noted voyage made within the same decade. Of about the same time are two French maps which Kohl reproduces for us, and on which the St. Lawrence for a considerable distance from its mouth, is fairly well drawn; but on one it is cut off, as being unknown further inland, while on the other it is represented as rising in mountains.

On the map of 1554 by John Bellero, there are several features worthy of notice, as for instance that the Amazon is represented as rising in Patagonia, and flowing northeast into the Atlantic, the whole with the name 'R. de esclavos.' In Central America appear 'Quatimala' and 'Nicaragua.' The name Florida appears twice, being applied in one case to the peninsula alone, and in the other, apparently to the entire territory north of the Gulf of Mexico. This map was exceedingly popular; was published in connection with two works this same year (1554), and repeated many times within the following fifteen years. On the almost equally celebrated map of Ramusio of 1556, the southern part of South America is occupied by the province of " Chili," out of which flows the " Rio Maragnon" northeastward, with its mouth at the equator.[1] The territory to the west of it is designated " El Peru," and that to the East, " Brazil." In the neighborhood of the city of Mexico stands the name 'Tecoantepech,' evidently the Tehuantepec of our day. The names of the principal places of Peru already appear; and we find on this map Trugillo [Truxillo], Lima, Acèquipa [Arequipa], Cusco, and a 'Chili' in smaller letters than those which seem to apply to the whole of the southern portion of the continent. One noteworthy feature of the map is that, according to Mr. Bancroft, it " is the first printed representation of North America as it was actually known; that is, with indications of a broad continent, but all left blank beyond the points of discovery." On the Zaltieri map of 1566, the interior is elaborated to an unusual extent. In Canada the " R. S. Lorenzo " flows southeast out of " Lago;" and near it are the localities " Ochelaza " and " Ochelai." To the south is " Larcadia," and west of this stands " Terra di Norumbega." The whole interior is filled with Mountains; and a range in the northwest receives the name " Apalchen," out of which form has evidently been developed the present name of the eastern mountain range of the United States, Appalachian. " Granata " is the general name on this map for the region later known as New Mexico; and several towns are indicated, but none of those now existing. Mexico is well supplied with names, among which are noted " Temistitain " and " Mistecui," probably Italianized forms of Temixtitlan and Mexico. On the Ortelius map of 1570, with all its richness of detail, and large measure of accuracy, there is a confused representation of the Amazon which is striking. Between the equator and the twentieth parallel south there are drawn two large rivers, rising in the

---

[1] The river is similarly represented on the Furlani map of 1560.

Andes, and flowing in almost parallel courses toward the east, and connecting in the middle. The northern one is called " Amazonum uel Oregliana fl.," and the southern one, " Maragnon." Near the mouth of the latter is the inscription: *"Rio Maragnone cuius ostium distat ab ostio Amazonis fl. 104 leucis teste Theuto."* How this confusion arose it would be interesting to know; but it is not here the place to go into possible explanations, none of which would be better than conjecture. On the Judaeis map of 1593 are to be found some interesting statements, as in the far west: *"In his montibus habitant diversae nationes qui continuis bellis inter se conflictantur: Avanares, Albardi, Calicuas, Tagil, Apalchen pluresque aliae."* The eastern part of the territory now occupied by the United States is divided into " Francia Nova," ' Virginia,' and ' Carolina.' In Virginia a mountain range running east and west has near it the name ' Apalchen,' while the mountains separating this English territory from the French one of Carolina, bear the inscription *"Apalatei montes in quibus aurum et argentum."* Quite a number of local names occur both in the east and west, and Canada is fairly well represented. The latter half of the sixteenth century was on the whole rather barren of results in the growth of geographical knowledge of America, and we find very little that is new, either in books of description or on the maps.

The opening of the seventeenth century saw the establishment of a permanent French settlement in Canada, and a lasting colony of English planted in Virginia ; and from these two centres explorations into the interior were made, and maps thereof drawn, so that from this time on we see the continual growth of the inland geography of the main portion of the northern continent. The French penetrated to the north and west of the head waters of the St. Lawrence, brought to light the Great Lakes and the Rocky Mountains beyond, and did also some exploring in the present New England, where they came into collision with the English. The intrepid John Smith, setting out from the struggling colony of Jamestown, explored the waters of the neighboring bay and rivers, and the Atlantic coast-line up through New England. French exploration went on more rapidly than the English, because of the religious zeal of the former's monastic orders. On the other hand, the English colonists had come to stay and make homes for themselves; and, with the exception of such rare enthusiastic spirits as John Smith, they did but little exploring merely for the sake of seeing the country, when they were not seeking a place to found a new colony. Before the middle of the century, the sea-board between the French on the north and Virginia on the south was occupied by several colonies from the Netherlands and Sweden, as well as from England; and the general maps soon began to show something of a political aspect. Already on the map published by Hakluyt in 1589 there was an attempt to draw boundary lines, the first map on which we have observed anything of the kind. In North America there are only four divisions:—1, the great northwest, containing the legend 'America sive India Nova;' 2, to the northeast was 'Nova Francia;' 3, south of this, 'Florida,' and the remainder to the isthmus 'Hispania noua.' South America is divided into five great provinces: 'Caribana' in the north; 'Humos Brasi,' from the mouth of the Amazon east; 'Chiba' in the south; 'Peru' in the west; while the centre, between the middle Amazon and the Plata, received the name 'Amazones.' The second map of this nature, known to us, is a French map of about 1640, the original of which is in the Dépôt de la Marine of Paris. This is a rude map without lines of latitude and longitude, and the coast-lines by no means accurately drawn; but it is interesting as showing the conception of the division of the continent, at that time probably accepted by the French. The basin of the St. Lawrence, which forms by far the largest part of the map, has no specific name. Far to the northwest is the "Lac des hurons," out of which a river flows toward the southeast, which empties into the St. Lawrence just east of the 'lac s louis.' Southwest from the latter are 'lac francois,' 'lac ontario' and

'Lac erie.' 'Lac Champlain' is also given, much distorted in form. From the Gulf of St. Lawrence, the Atlantic coast stretches almost due west, is indented with bays and rivers, and the whole territory divided into six districts, which, beginning in the east, are designated as follows :—" lacadia," " la nouuelle angleterre," " la nouuelle holande," " la nouuelle suede," " la uirginie," and " la floride." These are all marked off, the one from the other, by definite lines, and a mountain range separates them on the north from Canada. We may as well here note a peculiar feature of this map, which recurs on a number of other early maps, that is the fact that a continuous watercourse connects the Atlantic, on the New England coast, with the river St. Lawrence. We see thus the rude beginnings of political geography, that side of the science which at present attracts the most popular attention. It seems hard to realize that the vast territory, the political aspect of which could, two hundred and fifty years ago, be sufficiently represented in such crude form, is now filled with an immense population ; and that a good map of it should represent innumerable boundary lines of country, state, and county ; and contain hundreds of dots showing the situation of as many cities, towns, and villages.

As early as 1609 we find a map of Lescarbot, giving some of the political features of Canada ; for instance, " Kebec " appears for the first time, and there are also "Saincte Croix," " Sagenay," " Hochelaga," etc. For the town last named there is on the map a drawing of five houses within a stockade, the whole surmounted by the French *fleur-de-lis.* The river Kennebec is called " Kinibeki," probably the native name as the French understood it, from which the present form has been abridged. The French discovery of the Iroquois Indians is here brought to light, and the name is used twice, as designating respectively a country and a river. The rivers of St. John and St. Croix are drawn almost parallel, and empty into the Bay of Fundy which is distorted ; their names are spelled, " R. S. Jan " and " Saincte Croix." In the 1625

edition of Purchas there is a very well drawn map of this
region, on which quite a number of names occur that are
not found on other maps, as Clyde and Twede for the St. John
and St. Croix respectively; Cape Cod receives its present
name and is better drawn than on any previous map noted.
The then new settlement of Plymouth is placed considerably
further north than Cape Cod. "De la war bay" is evidently
the Chesapeake, for into it flow the rivers on which are the
settlements of "James Citti" and "Henrico," while at its
mouth are capes Charles and "Henric." However, no other
bay is given as lying between this and the Hudson river.
"New Scotlande" includes all of the territory now occupied
by Nova Scotia and New Brunswick. On de Laet's map of
"Florida et Regiones Vicinae," of the same year, the interior
is well filled with Indian names of native villages, to which
are added those of European origin, such as "S. Augustin"
of Florida, "Charlesfort" near "Port Royal" in the present
South Carolina, etc. "Apalatcy Montes," and a district under
the name "Apalache" attract also our attention, because of
their evident relation to modern well known names. No. 91,
of the Kohl Collection, reproduces for us a curious map
extracted from a work published in 1628 under the title of
"The World encompassed by Sir Fr. Drake." Here New
England is placed northwest of New France, and the whole
continent is called "North America or Mexicana," probably
the greatest extent ever given the name Mexico, which, as
elsewhere remarked, was originally the name of only a
quarter or district of the capital city of the Aztecs. The
extreme northwestern part of the continent is styled "New
Brittayne," and in the northern part of South America
appears for the first time "Guiana;" "Bonos Ayres," also a
new name, is applied to a small affluent of La Plata.

Kohl gives us copies of three maps published in 1630 in
de Laet's work on the New World. These show extended
information on the part of their compiler, not only as to the
projects of settlement of his own country but also the work

4

in that direction done by other and rival nations. One of these maps is entitled "*Americae sive Indiae Occidentalis Tabula Generalis*," and the two continents are called respectively, "Septentrionalis Americae pars," and "Meridionalis Americae pars." "Tierra del Fuego" is cut off on the south with a dotted line, it being already known that there was open sea beyond it, since de Laet's countrymen had passed that way in 1616; but as they did not explore the islands in detail, the land's extent is here marked as unknown. Some idea of the Great Lakes had already penetrated to Europe, as the St. Lawrence River is here represented as rising in a lake to the northwest, which lake has no western bounds. Just west of "C. Cod," (which on one of the maps is called "C. Blanc"), the territory is called "Novum Belgium," while "Nova Anglia" is further north, and to the west of Nova Scotia. "R. Pentegouet" is evidently meant for Penobscot, though the name seems to be more nearly related to Pemaquid, also evidently an Indian name, which was applied to a settlement made about that time in this vicinity ; and "R. Quinibequi" is to us a new form of Kennebec. In such names as "Cadie," "Nieuw Engeland," "Vossen haven," [Boston Haven], "Hellegat," "Manbatte," [Manhatten], "Nieuw Nederland," "Noordt River,' "Zuyd River," we easily recognize old friends, dressed, however, in somewhat strange habiliments. South America also contains many names which by this time had come into more or less general use.

Champlain's map of 1632 is the work of a careful explorer who understood also how to depict what he had seen. The territory represented on this map is almost exclusively that visited by the draughtsman himself and included under the name Nouvelle France. The St. Lawrence rises in Lake St. Louis, west of which are two small lakes without names. To the northwest is shown an immense body of water under the name "Mer douce," with its greatest extent from east to west. This error continued for a long time to disfigure the maps of this region ; for the early explorers did not realize that Georgian Bay, though connected with, is not a part of Lake Huron. Still further west there is "Grand lac," evidently Lake Superior. Of course Lake Champlain is given, the special discovery of the maker of this map; but it is too broad for its length; and for Lake George there is represented a wide bay near the southwest end of the main lake; while the general trend of the whole is northeast and southwest, rather than north and south, as it is in reality. On the Maine coast is the settlement "Pemetegoit," probably Pemaquid, and further to the east, St. Croix; Quebec is spelled as now.

In the work of William Wood, entitled "New England's Prospect, a true, lively and experimental description of that part of America, commonly called New England," there is a map of "The South part of New England, as it is planted this yeare 1634." The degrees of latitude are marked on the eastern margin, and the city of Boston is placed at 42½ degrees, which is very accurate for that period, as the position is now put at 42° 22' [Scribner-Black Atlas, 1890]. On this map, an American begins to feel at home, when he encounters a considerable number of old familiar names, such as Salem, Roxbury, Charlestowne [applied to both settlement and river], Dorchester, Nantasket, Cohassett, 'Sitliate' [Scituate], New and Old Plymouth, 'Pascataque Riuer' [Piscataqua River], 'Islands of Shoulds' [Isles of Shoals], 'Merimock' River, Cape Ann, Marble Harbor, Nahant Point, 'Narrogansett's' bay and river, etc.

In "A relation of Maryland," published in 1635, there is a map of that region, with the west turned toward the top. "Chesapeack bay" is elaborately drawn, and extends fully up to the 40th degree of north latitude, while Delaware Bay is crudely represented, as if known only by hearsay, and, according to the scale given on the map itself, does not reach the 40th parallel by eight "Sea Leagues." Between the upper waters of the two bays is the name of a tribe of Indians, "Sasquehannocks," doubtless the origin of the name of Pennsylvania's long river, the Susquehanna. The chief river of the region as shown on the map is the "Patowmeck," at whose mouth is placed the then new settlement of Lord Baltimore, with the elaborate name of "St. Maries Augusta Catolina." The settled part of Virginia is also added to the map and the usual names given.

From the middle of the seventeenth century, the general features of the Atlantic sea-board were fairly well known in one part or another of Europe; and for the future we shall remark only such features of the maps that come under notice as are new, or for some other reason are of special interest. Immigration to the New World was now an established thing, and the stream, though not so mighty as it was in time to become, was already quite constant; and many there were, not only anxious to come for a time, for the sake of adventure or speculation, but who found here life more agreeable or at least more tolerable, than in the fatherland. It is not possible in geographical works to follow the gradual penetration of the wilderness by individual pioneers, how their families grew up about them, and friends and acquaintances were attracted thither, till in time a settlement was there, large enough to call attention to its existence. But such is the true historical development precedent to the growth of our geography, especially on its political side.

The second half of the century was a busy one in America; and while the English colonists were engaged in laying the foundations of a future great commonwealth, the French, in their self-sacrificing missionary labors, were bringing to light vast stretches of the continent, whose immensity till then had not even been dreamed of. All of the Great Lakes were soon on the maps, with a fair idea of their inter-connection; and the Mississippi, from its head-waters almost, even to its mouth in the Gulf of Mexico, was traversed and mapped, while the size of the streams flowing into it, furnished the first ground for estimating the immensity of the country drained by its waters. A French anonymous map of 1660 gives all the Great Lakes: "Lacus Ontarius," very well drawn; "Lac"

"Erius s. Felis," less so; "Lacus aquarum Marinarum," the name given to Lake St. Clair, which however is represented as only a slight broadening of the river; "Mare dulce seu Lacus Huronum," is Lake Huron, as usual much exaggerated in its breadth; "Lacus Superior" is not known as far as its western extremity; only the northeastern portion of Lake Michigan is depicted, and bears the legend "Magnus lacus Algonquinorum seu Lacus Faetentium." This map shows also an acquaintance on the part of the French, with the Virginia settlements, and also with the Swedish settlements on the Delaware. Of about ten years later is another anonymous French map with the title "Lac Superieur, et autres lieux, où sont les Missions des Pères de la Compagnie de Jesus," etc. Here the entire lake is represented, and bears the name of Tracy as well as its more usual and now universal one of Superior. It is drawn too long, by about 100 miles, according to the scale; but when we consider that this is the first attempt, as far as we know, to represent this entire body of water, and that the only survey thereof had been a crude reconnaissance, we must rank the work as of high quality. Lake Michigan has the name "Lac des Illinois;" and near the junction of the lakes we find the beginnings of the modern towns of Ignace and Mackinaw, under the term missions.

Kohl gives in No. 227 of his collection a map which he believes to be a copy of the one which Father Marquette himself made during his voyage on the Mississippi in 1673. The latitude is marked on the margins, and includes the territory from the 32d to the 48th degree north. Here are met some strange-looking names, which, however, have evidently connection with some well-known modern ones. The Missouri river is not named, but near it is placed a tribe of Indians with the name "Oumesourit;" while not far off is another tribe named "Kansa." At the junction of the Mississippi, with an unnamed river which is probably the Arkansas, is another tribe of Indians called "Arkansea." On the Ohio River is found "R. Ouabouskiaou," which, according to Kohl, is the original of our Wabash. "Kachkaska" is a small stream flowing east into the southwestern corner of the "Lac des Illinois;" a name that is doubtless Kaskaskia, and since that time transferred to a river in the southern part of Illinois, which flows into the Mississippi. Another map of the same year is extracted from Thevenot's work of Voyages and Travels, and represents the same region. On the first map the Mississippi bore the name Conception, while it here receives a name recognizable as related with its modern one, "Mitchisipi ou Grande Riviere." The latitude of most places is wrongly represented, and no attempt is made to give their longitude. The map bears also a less number of recognizable names. Worthy of remark is the fact that, during his voyage, Marquette was told by the Indians that beyond the source of the Missouri, there rose another river which flows westward,— probably the first intimation on this side the Rocky Mountains of the existence of the Columbia River. Of two years later is the Joliet map of the Mississippi valley, which region is called on the map "La Colbertie ou Amerique Occidentale ;" and the Father of Waters itself is named after the Frenchman Colbert. The Allegheny and Ohio Rivers are not named, but bear the legend "Riviere par ou descendit Le Sieur de la Salle au sortir du Lac Erie pour aller dans le Mexique." Niagara Falls receive the striking name "Sault de demi lieue." On another map made by Joliet, probably during the following decade, the head waters of the Mississipi are placed in about 54 degrees of north latitude, and the name has become modified to "Messisipi." Of about the same period is a map of Raffeix on which we meet for the first time "Ohoio La belle Riviere." Father Hennepin's map of 1683 gives us "La Louisiane" for the first time, and applies to some of the Great Lakes names not elsewhere met with.

But detail grows perhaps wearisome, and to continue the geographical history of the United States at the same rate would fill a volume, instead of being part of an hour's lecture. The subject in itself, however, cannot fail to be interesting to any one who desires to know the development of his country.

Before the close of the seventeenth century there was in Europe a knowledge of the general features of the territory of the United States, with the exception of the far northwest; and during the eighteenth century, this knowledge was somewhat increased in detail. Veranderie succeeded in penetrating west from Lake Superior to the Rocky Mountains; and Le Page du Pratz relates the story of an Indian named Moncacht Apé, who in 1745 made his way over the mountains, and descended the "Beautiful River," as he called the stream on whose waters he voyaged to the Pacific. We are not accustomed to think of Indians as explorers, who leave their homes and wander several thousand miles merely for the sake of gratifying their curiosity. However, there seems little room for doubt in reference to this first recorded exploration of the Pacific slope by any one coming from the country east of the Mississippi. But the eighteenth century did on the whole very little toward opening up the vast interior of this great continent to the knowledge of civilized man; and we pass accordingly to the beginning of the present century, when the then young and zealous federal government, under the lead of Jefferson, purchased Louisiana, and sent out explorers to report on the territory which had thus come into our possession. These opened the way, which hardy pioneers seeking for homes were not slow to follow; and what was thus begun was accelerated by the discovery of gold, as the middle of the century drew near. This fact has had more effect in a few decades than mere human curiosity to penetrate the secrets of nature had had in as many centuries. Look upon a map of the great West, of the last century or of only half a century ago, and on one of the present day, and behold the evidences of the work of man; for nature during that period has remained practically the same, and all the immeasurable difference there observable is due to human energy.

Polar Chorography.

We turn now to a region which, though among the earliest portions of the New World to attract attention, is the last to be well known, because of the inherent difficulties of exploring it. Here is the one part of the earth where a love of science has been to a large extent the moving factor in its exploration, and where wealth and life itself have been offered up in the most generous manner in order to bring to us a knowledge of it. From the suggestion of Cabot in the fifteenth century to the present, interest therein has sometimes been at a low ebb, but never for any length of time been entirely wanting. Here is the region also where imagination has played the greatest rôle; and much of the geographical representation of which is purely the product of fertile brains without any foundation in fact or experience. Something of this feature has been told in treating of the Pacific coast; and in the short time at our disposal now, it will be better to confine the attention to the facts of the case as shown on various relatively trustworthy maps.

The first explorers of the frigid regions of the Atlantic were, however, not actuated by any higher motives than those of commercial gain; for they desired to reach the wealth of the Orient by a passage which could not be blocked by the Portuguese, who by right of first discovery and by the gift of the Holy See, had the sole title to the route *via* the Cape of Good Hope. Furthermore,. if found, the route by the northwest passage would be much shorter, especially for the nations of northern Enrope, than that around Africa. Though much of this region was doubtless known to the Northmen from the eleventh to the fourteenth century, no maps of that period are known to us, except that of the Italian, Zeno, of the fourteenth century, which however, was not given to the world till the year 1558. This map contains a variety of names, some of which were reproduced on maps down to a comparatively late period; and about the signification of which there

has been a great deal of learned dispute. Probably as rational
interpretation of these names as we can find is that of Major,
who has made a careful study of the matter. He gives the
modern equivalents of the names as follows: 'Engroelant,'
Greenland; 'Islanda,' Iceland; 'Estland,' the Shetland
Islands; 'Frisland,' Faroe Islands; 'Markland,' Nova Scotia;
'Estotiland,' Newfoundland; 'Drogeo,' coast of North
America; 'Icaria,' coast of Kerry in Ireland.

As of Columbus's first voyage, so of Cabot's, there remains
no map to tell us just where he saw the American coast.
Years later Sebastian Cabot made a map of the New World,
which, however, attempts to portray all that was known up to
the time of drawing it; so that there are no means of ascertain-
ing just what had been discovered by his father or himself. The
oldest map which represents the northeastern part of North
America, and belonging to what may be called the Columbian
period of discovery, in contradistinction to that of the Northmen, is the Cantino map of 1502, which shows early Portuguese discoveries in the north. On another Portuguese map,
of 1504, we find "Newfoundland and Labrador under the
name of 'Terra de Cortte Reall,' and Greenland with no name,
but so correctly represented as to form strong evidence that
it was reached by Cortereal" [H. H. Bancroft]. This is the
most accurate map of that region which appeared for a long
time. Those in the editions of Ptolemy of 1508 and 1511 are
not at all well drawn as regards this portion; and even as late as
the Schoener globe of 1520, not as much is known in Germany
of this region as is depicted on this early Portuguese map. This
state of the case continued until the English explorations were
renewed in the last quarter of the sixteenth century. In the
meantime Zaltieri in 1566 and Ortelius in 1570 had made an
approach toward a fair representation of the northern regions;
but whether these were the result of surmises on their part or
whether they knew of explorations in those parts, of which
we have no records, I cannot say. In 1578 appeared George
Best's "A true discourse of the late voyages of discoveries, for"

"the finding of a passage to Cathaya by the North West under the conduct of Martin Frobisher, generall, . . ." In this work there is a map of the world in the form of a flattened ellipse, the most northerly part of which is occupied by four immense islands, bearing the title "Terra Septentrionalis." South of the western half of these are "Frobishers Straights," the eastern portion of which contains a group of islands that Frobisher himself called Terra Incognita. On Dee's map of 1580 the polar regions receive careful treatment, and the strait discovered by Frobisher is well represented ; but is continued inland, to an indefinite extent. Here are also some of the names of the Zeno map. The Lok map of two years later shows much more evidence of actual acquaintance with the region, though the knowledge has by no means yet become accurate. Frisland is here a peninsula in the far northeast, extending below the 60th parallel, while 'Island' is just north of 'Hibernia,' on the Arctic Circle. 'Groenland' is all above the circle, extending almost to 80 degrees north. To the northwest of this there is also 'Iac. Scolvus Groetland.' Frobisher Strait, Lok Island, and other names also appear.

In 1585, 1586, and 1587, John Davis made his celebrated arctic voyages, and opened up much new territory to the knowledge of the English ; but I have seen no map from his hand, or that is the direct product of his discoveries. Certainly, the map of the world, by Iohannes Myrtius, contained in a book bearing the date 1590, whose introduction is dated 1587, contains no glimmer of such information. Hakluyt's map of 1589 takes but little notice of any English discoveries in the far north, and continues the already known strait westward into the Pacific. Of the other discoveries, there is no trace. Wytfliet's map of 1597 has at 60 degrees north a "Golfo de Merosro," southwest of which is placed "Terra Corterealis," "which," says Kohl, "supports the old tradition, that Cortereal entered a strait or gulf in that latitude, and that this Gulf of Cortereal was our Hudson's Strait." On Hakluyt's later map, of 1598, are located both "Fretum Davis" and

" Frobisher's Straights;" and south of the latter is "Estotiland." The map in Purchas, 1625, begins to bear some
resemblance in the north to our present conception of that
country. "Fretum Hudson" leads west to Hudson Bay;
and the western part of the latter is called "Button Baie,"
with the connecting shore between them still omitted. To the
northeast is "Parte of Groenland, with "C. Farewell" at its
southern extremity, and "Fretum Davis" separating it from
the mainland. On the English map, extracted from the work
on the voyage of Francis Drake, there is added to what we
have noted on the other maps, "Baffin's Bay," which had
been discovered sixteen years before by the man whose name
it bears. Of the year 1631 there is a work devoted to the
description of the voyage of the discoverer of James Bay,
accompanied by a good map of the region visited.

From this time on, to the beginning of the present century,
there was but little done toward bringing to light the secrets of
this vast country, forever under the rule of winter. But the
valuable work of Sir John Franklin, in connection with his
tragic fate, reopened the subject in the first half of our century; and since then the various nations of the civilized world
have vied with each other in their efforts to penetrate the veil
that hitherto has concealed this country from view. A great
complex of islands and numerous water ways have been mapped for us, the limits of the mainland designated, and the
fact established that a water communication between the Atlantic and Pacific does exist here; but all hope has been
abandoned that it will ever, at least in our era, prove practicable for commerce. Fortunately the need for it has long since
disappeared, and the high seas have become free as the air to
all who trust themselves to their treacherous waves.

IV.

HISTORICAL NOTES ON CERTAIN GEOGRAPHICAL NAMES.

America.

The discovery of a New World has made Columbus the hero of centuries, and his name has been mentioned with almost universal praise. The maps however, give no prominence to that name, but bear in large letters the name of another; and both he who bore this name in life, and he who proposed its adoption in the world's geography, have been decried and execrated almost as much as lauded. How have such anomalies come about? To Clio we must look for the answer; but, though the roll she bears in her hand contains all truth, she never lets any one individual see the whole; and accordingly accounts differ as to what men have there found. We must therefore not expect the absolute, unalterable truth in applying to History for an explanation of the past; but, examining such fragments as she offers to our view, judge of their contents in a manner consistent with the most probable solution of the problem to which we apply ourselves. In the present case the contest lies between Spain and Germany; between a country that strove to grasp all in secrecy, and one whose subjects remained at home and sought to diffuse knowledge; between the sword and the pen : and, as history has so often demonstrated, the pen, in this case also, was the stronger. Recently there has developed another struggle, based on the fact that theorists have arisen who are trying to destroy the authenticity of the records of the centuries, and who find the name America a product of the

60

land that bears it, and not a latinized form of the name of a man who has been branded as a braggart and an impostor.

Columbus started out in 1492 to find, not a New World, but the Asia which Marco Polo had described in such glowing terms, and whose riches and spices were valuable beyond measure. Though he came to the western hemisphere four times and touched the continent of America twice, he lived and died in the belief that he had visited the eastern part of Asia. He was told of the existence of the Pacific Ocean, but in his blindness, gave the information another interpretation. He saw little or nothing such as Marco Polo had described, yet he compelled his companions to swear that they believed themselves on the coast of Asia. He tried to have his discoveries kept secret even from his fellow countrymen, and his government attempted to prevent the knowledge passing outside their realms ; so that when the rest of the world had any information of the new discoveries, they were at liberty to apply to the regions known such names as pleased their fancy. Columbus claimed for himself wealth and political power as the reward of his discovery, and died poor and neglected, though his descendants received what he had desired. But another visited these shores, with facile pen in hand, and gave to the world through his friends and patrons a glowing description of the beauties and wonders his eyes had beheld in that strange country ; and added " *Novum mundum appellare licet ;* " and for a long time it was so called : but as in the case of Magellan, the name which he proposed for the strait of his discovery gradually gave way to his own name, so in this other case, the name proposed by Americus Vespucius gradually made room for his own name. Though Vespucius was not probably the original discoverer of the coast of South America, he was the first to tell the world what an extensive and magnificent country it is ; and a world, grateful for the information, and liking the sound of the name, adopted it. As he was a foreigner, the Spaniards were long unwilling to receive that appellation ; but though they could conquer the greatest part of the New World, they did not in the end have the privilege of naming it: and their selfish secrecy is, in our humble opinion, the prime cause of the fact.

Inasmuch as Columbus believed that he was sailing in the waters of Asia, he had no reason to seek a new name for the whole extent of territory which he visited; moreover, he did not see nearly so much of the mainland as in all probability Vespucius did; and for local names he was content to apply the names of saints, or a name suggested by his experience at a given point, or even to adopt the native name, as he understood it from the mouths of the Indians. Vespucius may still have thought this to be a part of Asia; but he evidently recognized the difference between what he saw and what he had expected to see in the land of Marco Polo; and in all earnestness he proposed the name New World for this enormous extent of country; and even the Spaniards accepted his proposition.

There are grave discrepancies in the accounts we have of the life of Vespucius, and also in his own accounts of his voyages to America. But that seems to us to have little to do with the acceptance of his name for the western continents. If it comes to a question as to the justness of so honoring him above Columbus, then even if he had seen the continent a year or so earlier than the great admiral, it would be unjust to give him the preference; for there can be little doubt that he would never have visited the western hemisphere if Columbus had not shown the way. But the two men were of entirely different moulds; and the result is in accordance therewith. The one sought immediate power and wealth; and largely by his own mismanagement failed; but the justness of history has given him his due theoretically, while helpless to alter the habits of men; the other sought notoriety by the aid of his pen; the world read, was interested and entertained, and formed the habit of speaking of the region and the man who first revealed it, in the same breath; and as man is a creature of habit, the name will probably endure as long as the race which now inhabits the continent. The history of geography shows that the names of the prominent features of a land are most enduring, as witness the names of the Mississippi River, the Ohio, Missouri, and others, names used by the Indians who have long since been gathered to their fathers; and whose descendants, if there be any, are living far away from the graves of their ancestors. If they had possessed a general name for the entire continent, that, too, would perhaps, nay, probably, have been preserved to this day; but as that was lacking, and another, convenient and euphonius, was proposed, it was accepted and will probably endure for untold ages to come.

In the year following the death of Columbus, there was published in a small town of Lorraine, a work of but fifty-two small quarto pages, which contained a proposition, modestly worded, but which was to result in naming the great stretch of land that occupies the western hemisphere. This pamphlet bore the title *Cosmographiae Introdvctio. . . . Insuper quatuor Americi Vespucij Nauigationes.* It is said to have been the first complete edition of the writings of Vespucius on the New World, although portions of them had appeared earlier. These writings were destined to become popular; and before 1530 there were issued in French, German, Italian, and Latin at least fourteen editions of them. The important passage for us in this work reads in English as follows:—
"But now that those parts have been more extensively examined, and another fourth part has been discovered by Americus (as will be seen in the sequel), I do not see why we should rightly refuse to name it America, namely, the land of Americus or America, after its discoverer, Americus, a man of sagacious mind, since both Europe and Asia took their names from women." (H. H. Bancroft.)[1] If those had been days

---

[1] The original as given by Peschel [Abhandlungen zur Erd- und Völkerkunde, 231-2], reads:—"*Nunc vero et hae partes [Europa, Africa, Asia] sunt latius lustratæ et alia quarta pars per Americum Vespucium (ut in sequentibus audietur) inventa est, quam non video cur quis jure vetet ab Americo inventore, sagacis ingenii viro Amerigen quasi Americi terram sive Americam dicendam: cum et Europa et Asia a mulieribus sua sortita sint nomina.*"

when newspaper notoriety could be purchased for money, there
might be some foundation for the modern accusation that
Vespucius was in collusion with the editor, and so responsible
for depriving Columbus of the honor of having his name
attached to the world he had discovered; but if that had been
the case, he would probably have chosen some other press for
the propagation of his scheme, than a comparatively obscure
one far away from the centre of exploring activity. The
ruling duke of Lorraine happened to be a promotor of learning, and had gathered at the little town of St. Dié a small
company of learned men to conduct the local university, one
of whom was especially interested in geography, and another
of whom had studied in Paris and possibly met a personal
friend of Vespucius. These men planned the issue of a new
edition of the geographical work of Ptolemy, and made their
preparations accordingly. As a preliminary, this little *Introdvctio* was published on the 25th of April, 1507; but the
main work was interrupted by the death of the patron duke,
and the Ptolemy was not issued till 1513, and was then
printed in Strasburg. Furthermore, the map of America in
that Atlas does not bear the name America. In the meantime,
Vespucius had died, having lived on cordial terms with the
family of Columbus, although there had continued for several
years a suit at law between that family and the Spanish Court
in reference to the first discovery of the northern coast of
South America; in which, however, Vespucius made no claim
to be the first discoverer, notwithstanding the fact that the
work of Hylacomylus was known in Spain and Columbus'
son possessed a copy of the same, wherein the statement occurs
that Vespucius had made a voyage to the mainland in the
year 1497. This statement has been interpreted to mean
North and Central America, and there is a bare possibility of
his having made such a voyage; but there is no evidence that
he himself, then or at any period of his life, laid claim to be the
original discoverer of the continent. All of his so-called four
voyages have been declared by his assailants to be apocryphal,

although three have been proven beyond reasonable doubt, to be authentic. This relieves him of the charge of being an impostor; and it may yet possibly be shown that the first voyage also was really made. At least the contrary has not been proven. However, Santarem "claims that one hundred thousand documents in the Royal Archives of Portugal, and the register of maps which belonged to King Emmanuel, make no mention of Vespucius, and that there is no register of the letters patent which Vespucius claimed to have received. Nor is there any mention in several hundred other contemporary manuscripts preserved in the great library at Paris, and in other collections, which Santarem says he has examined." (Winsor.) As he is bitterly hostile to the fame of Vespucius, these sweeping statements should probably be received with some allowance. Mr. Gay, in Winsor's Narrative and Critical History, gives form to an idea that the name was originally meant to be applied only to that country surrounding a settlement which Vespucius established near Cape Frio, and that by the force of circumstances, this name came to be applied to the whole continent. He says :—" The precise spot of this settlement is uncertain ; but as it was planted by Vespucci, and as it was the first colony of Europeans in that part of the New World, there was an evident and just propriety in bestowing the derivative—America—of his name upon the country, which at first was known as 'The Land of the True Cross,' and afterward as ' Brazil.' The name of Brazil was retained when the wider application—America—was given to the whole continent." (II. 152.) That this is a possible solution of the difficulty can be shown from analogous cases in the history of America. Thus Cartier gave the name St. Lawrence to a little bay near the mouth of the St. Lawrence River; and the gradual change from that application to the whole Gulf and River which now bear the name can be traced on the maps. Likewise we have the authority of Kohl for the statement that Gautimala was originally the name of the city and residence of a powerful cacique in southeastern Mexico, to which district

5

Cortes had sent Alvarado in 1523; and the name occurs in the latter's report of his expedition to his general; furthermore, that at one time, almost all of Central America was under the *"Audiencia"* or general government of that name. Still more striking is the name of Mexico, which at first was applied to only a district of the capital city of Montezuma, and was gradually enlarged in its application, till it embraced the whole country.

We can scarcely realize in these days of newspapers and the publication of thousands of books annually, that before the year 1507 only two descriptions of the western discoveries had appeared, namely, one letter of Columbus, and one of Vespucius. No wonder then that a curious public eagerly bought Waldseemuller's little quarto, and called for four editions of the same in a short time; no wonder that, by perusing it, the public was lead to believe that Vespucius was the great discoverer. Can it then seem strange to us that the Germans at least were willing to attach his name to the country of which they had first heard through his writings alone? It has generally been supposed that the earliest map to bear the name America was that of Apianus or Bienewitz, of the year 1520, which appeared in an edition of the geographical work of Solinus, published in Vienna in 1522. Of the same period is the Nuremberg globe of Schoener (1520), whereon the name America also occurs. Then there is a map, long ascribed to Leonardo da Vinci, and now in the queen's collection at Windsor, and thought to be of the year 1513 or 1514, whereon the name is drawn; but the date of the map is uncertain, and Winsor says: " Its connection with Da Vinci is now denied." On the other hand there is in the possession of Mr. Kalbfleisch of New York, an anonymous " *Cosmographiae Introductio,*" thought by the critics to be of the year 1517, in which there is a map with the name America, of which Mr. Winsor remarks: " There is fair ground for supposing that it antedates all other printed maps yet known which bear this name." The same author believes the Frankfort globe of 1515 to be the first drawing on which the name occurs.

Upon the map by Apianus, the name is situated along the eastern coast of Brazil, south of Cape Augustine, and reads "*America provincia;*" and on Schoener's globe of 1520 it reads "*America vel Brasilia sive Papagalli terra;*" thus showing, as Mr. Gay suggests, that it was originally intended to apply the name only to that portion of the country where Vespucius had been, and in whose neighborhood he may have attempted to found a colony. That the name was not rapidly adopted, we gather from the assertion of Peschel that, of twenty-two editions of Ptolemy's tables that were issued during the sixteenth century, the name America is nowhere found; but Mr. Winsor assures us that the name occurs in the Ptolemy of 1522. The Germans, however, stood by their countryman, in upholding his proposition; and on Mercator's map of 1541 the name America is applied, for the first time we believe, to both continents of the western hemisphere; and, in the words of Mr. Winsor, "thus the injustice was made perpetual." As early as 1519 or 1520 there was a book published in London with the title New Interlude, in a verse of which the name America occurs; and not long after, (1522) appeared the first English book to treat of America, which however it called "Armenica." It is entitled "Of the newe lādes and of ye people founde by the Messengers of the Kynge of portygale." This same year Friess issued his "*Orbis typus universalis,*" etc.; and on the map showing his conception of the New World, the name America is found designating the continent of South America. Apianus published in 1524 a "*Cosmographicus Liber,*" which contains a short chapter on America, in which he makes the direct statement that the land was named from Vespucci, its discoverer. (H. H. Bancroft.)

The Spanish maps of 1527 and 1529, so frequently mentioned already, both designate South America by the name *Novus Mundus*, the name, as we have seen, proposed by Vespucius himself. Among the Spaniards this name alternated with New

Indies and West Indies; as they were for a long time unwilling to accept the German usage. Las Casas in his Historia, begun in 1527, shows that he knew of the German usage, for he says: "Foreign writers call the country America." (Quoted, Winsor, II, p. 174). The Spaniards then began to propose other names, which, however, never had any currency; such as Colonia, Columbiana, and Columba; while one enthusiast went so far as to wish to unite the names of the sovereigns, under whom Columbus made his voyage of discovery, in the awkward compound Fer-Isabelica. Cabral had named the stretch of the Brazilian coast seen by him, Land of the True Cross; and that, or more commonly, Land of the Holy Cross, continued for some time to adorn the Spanish maps, but was finally superseded by the shorter and more euphonious name America.

On an anonymous map of about 1530, and the Grynaeus map of 1531, America is the name given to South America; and in 1532 appeared the *Novus Orbis* of this same Grynaeus, in which "the assertion is made that Vespucci discovered America before Columbus, which aroused the wrath of Las Casas, and seems to have originated the subsequent bitter attacks on Vespucci." (H. H. Bancroft.) About the middle of the century, we find on the Nancy globe and on a map in the work of Friess, the name America; but though in South America, it is in neither case given any very great prominence.

In 1570 was published Ortelius' atlas, the first product of modern times worthy the name. It contained a map of the New World which became the model of many succeeding ones; and, as it bore the name America, it brought that name into such general use that it could not thereafter be gotten rid of. The influence thus exercised was greatly strengthened by the issue of Mercator's atlas in 1598. These two men, the greatest geographers of their age, were friends; and their united influence in spreading this name for the New World surpassed the power of Spain or any other nation to root it out. Of course we must recognize the fact that its euphonious sound, and its analogy to the names of the other continents, were also not without effect; but just therein lay a part of their good judgment in giving their adhesion to an idea which of itself was likely to attract the masses as well as thoughtful men. A map of 1575 by Thomas Porcacchi da Castiglione bears the title *Mondo Nvovo ;* but in his remarks he says that some called it the "American Indies," a name we have not elsewhere noticed. On Sir Humphrey Gilbert's map of the following year, the name America is applied exclusively to North America, and Peru is apparently given to the whole of South America. Martin Frobisher, on his map of 1578, gives America in letters of the same size as Europe, Asia, etc. ; and evidently intends to use the name for the whole western mainland. Hakluyt's map of 1589 has the title *America sive India Nova,* which is doubtless intended for the entire continent.

On the map by Hondius, of the same year, AMERICA is placed in large capitals in North America ; and South America is divided into provinces, each with its own local name; but it is probable that, less of the interior of North America being known, he took occasion thus to fill it up with the name intended for the whole. Still another map of this same year, that of Judaeus, employs the name, and that in a somewhat new manner, having ' *Terra America* ' in North America ; and on a later map, the same author calls North America '*Americae pars borealis.*' The following year produced a map with titles for the two continents, which so far as we know, are almost unique; for Petrus Plancius calls North America, '*America Mexicana,*' and the southern continent, '*America Peruana.*' The map of Johannes Oliva, published at Marseilles in 1613, compromises between the Spanish and German methods of naming the New World, and applies to North America '*America sive India Nova,*' and to South America, ' *Mondo nouo ;* ' the latter however in small letters, placed near the Plata River. The map in the 1625 edition of Purchas gives us '*America Septentrionalis ;* ' and in the text there is related a conversation in which Juan de Fuca speaks of "the Indies now called North America." On the map which accompanies "The World encompassed by Sir Francis Drake," there is a similarity to the usage noted above in connection with the map of Plancius, namely, the northern continent is called 'North America or Mexicana,' and the southern continent, 'Sovth America or Peru.' On De Laet's map of 1630 there is another slight variation of the name, the title reading '*Americae sive Indiae Occidentalis Tabula Generalis,*' while on the part occupied by the northern continent we read '*Septentrionalis Americae pars.*' Thus we have followed the development of the usage of the name proposed in an obscure town of Lorraine, for the northeastern coast of South America, until it was accepted by a large part if not the whole of the learned world, for the entire hemisphere; and which, by the addition of adjectives, gradually distinguished between the north and the south. The designation Central America is of late origin; and I have not seen it on any map antedating the present century.

The above is we believe the true historical genesis of the geographical term America; but it would not do to dismiss the subject without mentioning the fact that within recent years there have been broached two other theories which, if we had not direct, trustworthy, historical statements to the contrary, might have at least a show of plausibility. The first is that of Mr. Jules Marcou, and was published in the Atlantic Monthly in March, 1875, pp. 291 et seq. His fundamental proposition is as follows:— "*Americ, Amerrique,* or *Amerique* is the name in Nicaragua for the high land or mountain range that lies between Juigalpa and Libertad, in in the province of Chrontales, and which reaches on the one side into the country of the Carcas Indians, and on the other into that of the Ramas Indians." He then proceeds to show that words of similar ending are frequent in the native languages of Central America, and remarks on the tenacity with which local names survive, such as those of mountains, valleys, lakes,

and rivers. Turning then to the last voyage of Columbus, in which he visited the coast of Central America, and the fact of his having found stores of gold among the natives there, he believes that, to the question as to whence came such wealth, the natives must have replied " Americ." " We may suppose," adds Mr. Marcou, " that Columbo and his companions on their return to Europe, when relating their adventures, would boast of the rich gold mines they had discovered through the Indians of Nicaragua, and say they lay in the direction of Americ. This would make popular the word Americ, as the common designation of that part of the Indies in which the richest mines of gold in the New World were situated." He supposes, further, that the name gradually penetrated to the interior of the continent of Europe, till it reached the little town of St. Dié. But he offers not one particle of contemporaneous evidence that such was the case. True, there are often movements of historical importance of which it is impossible to follow the early steps; but surely, if this supposition of our author were correct, some one of the many Spanish documents of the time would contain at least a hint of the fact; and even those pronounced enemies of the name America, such as Navarrete and Muñoz, find not a trace of such. As to the original proposition to use the name, he asserts:—
" Hylacomylus of Saint Dié, ignorant of any printed account of these voyages but those of Albericus Vespucius,—published in Latin in 1505, and in German in 1506,—thought he saw in the Christian name Albericus the origin of this, for him, altered and corrupted word, Americ or Amerique, and . . . called this country by the only name among those of the navigators that had reached him, and which resembled the word Americ or Amerique." To this he adds that Hylacomylus knew only the forms Albericus and Alberico of Vespucius' name, in as much as the other forms Amerigo and Morigo existed only in Spanish documents that remained unpublished until many years after the death of Hylacomylus. But that this is probably not the case, is strongly indicated by

the text of Hylacomylus himself, who, in proposing the name, evidently sought a form similar to that of the other quarters of the globe, and himself employs the phrase *"Amerigen quasi Americi terram sive Americam dicendam."* The very fact of his using first the form *Amerigen* appears as if he recognized that that was more closely related to the original, but that he made the change for purposes of euphony.

Mr. Marcou is evidently too strong in his assertion as to the rarity of the name Amerigo, since we find that two centuries before this, Dante was familiar with the names of the Spanish poets Amerijo de Pecutiano and Amerijo de Belinoi. Since j and g were at that period used interchangeably, as we find for example in the work of Garcilaso de la Vega, it follows that the form Amerigo may very well have been known to Hylacomylus. As to the accent not having been the same, we find that America was made analogous by the Spaniards; for in the index of Barcia's great work the name is printed América.

Mr. Marcou makes a good point of the unusual use of the Christian name of the discoverer for a land, in which he asserts this case to be practically unique, except in the name of monarchs; but he loses sight of the desire of Hylacomylus to assimilate the name with those of the other continents; and he suggests that Vespucia, or some similar word, would have been far more natural, if the word Americ were not already known to the author. But Vespucci is not so euphonious or so easily pronounced as America; and these considerations doubtless had weight with the scholar of St. Dié. Another statement of this new theory is: "There can be little doubt that the word America was not only known but popularized to a certain extent, in the sea-ports of Spain, Portugal, and the Indies, or it would not have been thus at once accepted by universal consent, without discussion." That it was not accepted at once and without discussion has been sufficiently shown, we believe, in our treatment of the matter. He further says: "And it was employed and accepted without a thought of the pilot Alberico Vespuzio; it was a long time after that discussions arose among learned geographers, and that the gross mistake of Hylacomylus was imposed upon the world as truth." That the first part of this second statement is not true, is demonstrated by the fact that the name was so intimately associated with that of Vespucius, that Columbus was in danger of being thereby forgotten as the original discoverer: and.as above remarked, it was this fact that roused the wrath of Las Casas against the admirers of Vespucius, and opened the discussion, which has continued from that time to the present. That commencement was not however so long after the first publication of the St. Dié tract as one would be led to suppose by Mr. Marcou's assertion; for it was the work of Grynaeus, which appeared in 1532 that is supposed to have precipitated the discussion; and Las Casas died in 1556, so' that the discussion must have started between these dates. Furthermore, Las Casas was in a splendid position to know if the name originated in America or in St. Dié; for his father was a companion of Columbus on his first voyage, and he himself took part in the third voyage, and spent many years in the New World. The facts that he introduces into the discussion not a word or hint that the name was of native origin, and ascribes its use only to foreign writers, are at least strong negative evidence that the name was *not* " popularized, to a certain extent, in the sea-ports of Spain."

The most recent theory that has come to our notice is that entitled " Discovery of the Origin of the Name of America, by Thomas de St. Bris. New York, 1888. Abridged Popular Edition." This is an octavo pamphlet of 140 pages, with a number of illustrations which seem to us but little germain to the subject in hand. The style is obscure, and the author has a method of punctuation all his own. He gives a bibliography of 63 numbers, and quotes foreign authors in English in such a manner, that it is at times impossible to know positively whether he is translating literally, or interspersing his own ideas in the translation. These peculiarities of style are

unfortunate, as they naturally repel the reader from the examination of a work that is evidently the result of much research and thought. We have not had time to consult many references of the author; but as one was at hand, it was examined, and found to convey a very different meaning from that implied by Mr. de St. Bris. In note 3, p. 58, he says :—
" Many authors, unaware that America was the national name of the Southern Continent, could not understand the Spanish pioneers, who gave this name to several places on the coast, and cartographers hotly disputed the question ; as to which was correct, without finding that they all were *." The * refers to the bottom of the page where a note reads, " See Kohl, Maracapana." Referring to his bibliography, the only work of Kohl mentioned is " *Die beiden ältesten General-Karten von Amerika.*" No page is given in the note ; but on page 121 of the above-named work, under the heading Mara-capana we read as follows : " The name Marcapana appears on both our maps not only improperly spelled but also in a false position. The port ' Maracapana ' made known by Hojeda's [Ojeda's (?)] expedition lay west of Margarita and Cumana, and is perhaps the modern port of Barcelona. All the good later maps. . . . have also Maracapana in the west where Herrera placed it. According to Navarrete it should be our Puerto Cochima." [1] This passage gives us no ground for the assertion that the question was " hotly disputed," for it says that " all the good later maps " placed the name Maracapana in the same place. Neither does it even hint that both posi-tions were correct. Furthermore, we would call attention to the fact that Mr. de St. Bris separates the word Maraca-pana

---

[1] " Der Name Maracapana scheint auf unsern beiden Karten sowohl unrichtig geschrieben, als auch eine falsche Position erhalten zu haben. Der von der Expedition des Hojeda bekannte Hafen " Maracapana " lag westlich von Margarita und Cumana und ist vielleicht unser heutiger Hafen von Barcelona. Alle guten spätern Karten . . . haben auch das Maracapana dort im westen, wohin es Herrera versetzt. Nach Navarrete soll es unser Puerto Cochima sein."

into two parts, in order to strengthen the impression of his theory; but Kohl does not do so; and America is very far from being a form of Maracapana.

However, whether correct or not, our author's theory is interesting. His central idea is that the native name of the immense territory occupied by the so-called Peruvians and their allied and kindred nations, was a modified form of the name America; that this name was composed from the words *amaru,* the name of their holy symbol the cross, formed by a snake, their holy animal, and a stick; to which was added the word *ca,* meaning land. Thus *Amaruca,* or usually America, was the land of the holy animal. " We have, therefore, at the period of the Spanish pioneers, the South American continent, under two great Kingdoms, of one name, and probably only one government; in an advanced state of civilization, civilly if not morally." " The population of the Empire of Amaraca—which extended along the Pacific coast for three thousand miles—was estimated at twelve millions." In the course of the work, a considerable variety of names are quoted from different authors, all of which are interpreted as signifying America although the word in this, its permanent form, seems to have been nowhere found until the suggestion of St. Dié. This suggestion he attributes to Walter Ludd; and besides, he loses sight of the fact, that from that time on the form remained constant, as applied to the whole continent, though the local names, from which he derives it, continued to be variable. In addition to the use of the word Amaraca, with a great variety of prefixes and suffixes, we are told that Cax-Amalca, Tamaraka, Tamaragua, Aymarca, Aromaia, are all really America. The divergence in the methods of spelling is explained by the use of sign language among the natives; but that "every European spelled the name with different letters, which he supposed to be more correct than his neighbor, who was left to guess what was meant." He attempts to fortify his theory by quotations from Walter Raleigh, Alexander von Humboldt, and others; in fact from any source whatever, where a word in the least resembling America is employed. One of the extracts from Raleigh's account of Guiana reads as follows:—" For when the Spaniards con-quored the saide Empire of Peru, and had put to death Atabalipa, which had formerly caused his elder brother Guascar to be slaine, one of his younger brothers fled out of Peru, and tooke with him many thousands of those souldiers of the Empire, called Oreiones (noblemen), and with these, and many others which followed him, he vanquished al that tract and valley of America, situated between the rivers Orenoco and Amazon." In quoting this passage, de St. Bris claims that Walter Raleigh " is the only author who has—as far as we know—correctly given the native name of the coast of America, first visited by Columbus." We think, however, that our author here strains a point for the sake of his theory; for we do not believe that any one, not having such a theory to defend, would interpret the phrase "al that tract and valley of America," in any other manner than as designating the part of the whole continent of America, namely that between the Orinoco and Amazon, which the writer intended. The English language is often ambiguous in the use of the prep-osition *of*; and so it is just possible, though not at all proba-ble, that Raleigh meant the name America to be applied to the valley, and no more. We must take into account the fact that this book was written late in the sixteenth century, when the name America, as applied to the New World was no longer a novelty, at least in the north of Europe ; and would fall naturally from the pen of such a man as Raleigh, as the name of the whole and not of a comparatively small portion, or that lying between the Amazon and Orinoco. Remarking that Columbus expected to find Asia, and the names mentioned by Marco Polo, our author asserts that Moraca-pana " was a transformation of the name Amaraca-pana or America; in order to give it some resemblance to Mangi." This is really beyond credulity ; for if a man makes a change, for the sake of establishing a similarity, he would surely in such a case have altered the consonants and not the vowels; for we entirely fail to see that Morica is much more nearly related to Mangi than Amaraca. Another quotation which he gives purports to come from Humboldt, but he does not say from which work of that voluminous writer. However he asserts that "Bishop Geraldini, writing from the new lands in 1515, said clearly, in a letter addressed to Pope Leon X. 'That the *island* was larger than Europe and Asia, which the ignorant call Asia, and others America or Paria.'" Since Geraldini was not made Bishop till 1520, there is evidently an error here. For in as much as it is thought by the best scholars that the name America was not in use among the Spaniards at so early a date, it is of the utmost importance that the date be accurately known, even if the letter is as quoted. According to our author, it was not Hylacomylus that baptized America but the great emperor Charles V., of whom he says (p. 126), "It was only a just tribute, a golden debt of gratitude, to erect an everlasting monument, a gigantic historical statue, always on the lips of the universe, in honor of the late Vice-King and Lord High Admiral Don Christopher Columbus, by instructing his cartographer Gérard Mercater [*sic*], to write over the *entire southern continent*, His 'plus ultra,' a world on His crest, the name of America, where it appeared—so far as we know—for the first time in this atlas issued in 1541, to which was added the remark 'many still call it India.'" He gives no authority for this very remarkable statement; but in a foot note kindly informs us that "We have only been able to find circumstantial evidence that Mercater wrote the name of America over the Southern Continent by the King's command." ! As we have elsewhere seen, it was precisely on this map of Mercator's of 1541 that the name America was for the first time placed on *both* continents of the New World; so here again there is a decided historical flaw in our author's argument, to say nothing of his assertion in reference to the command of the emperor, based on "circumstantial evidence." Furthermore, the Emperor Charles V. was still living when

Las Casas made his attack on the name America; and if our author were correct as to this supposition, the fact would then have come out, and thus put an end to the controversy. One more argument of Mr. de St. Bris, and we have finished. " It is hardly possible," he says, " that people of education, would have attempted to propose a name for territory, in which they had not the slightest interest; unless they had assumed that the proposition had already been practically carried out, which they were led to suppose from the similarity of name." When we consider that printing was then a comparatively new art, and that book makers as individuals were in a manner set above those around them; when to this is added the fact that in St. Dié for the first time, an edition of the entire writings of Americus Vespucius was published, we may well conceive of the author believing he had hit upon a happy thought, which would be pleasing to both him, whose work he published and to his readers. De St. Bris asserts that " the Spaniards had their principalities of New Granada, New Castile, the West Indies, Golden Castles, in the western hemisphere, but they wanted a general name to include all these possessions." If this were true when Mercator came to make his map in 1541, and it is in this connection that the statement occurs, how much more was it true in 1507, when Hylacomylus made his proposition.

Brazil.[1]

The history of the use of the name Brazil as a geographical term is a strange one; for it was not always applied to the same territory, with greater or less extent, as in the case of most geographical names; nor was it a case of natural growth from a local to a general name, as was frequently the case in the New World. On the contrary, this name seems to have

---

[1] This chapter appeared in the April number of " *Modern Language Notes,*" 1890.

had something of the will-o'-the-wisp character; for on various maps it may be seen designating a great Antarctic continent, extending to the south pole, or a small island near the Arctic Circle; or it may be as far west as the southern part of South America or as far east as the vicinity of the coast of Ireland. The form of the name also is almost as various as the positions in which it is found; for we have noted thirteen variations of the word, Bresilia, Brisilia, Brasil, Brassil, Brazil, Brazill, Prisilia, Brasilia, Brasielie, Brazili, Brazile, Brasi, Presilly,—and it is not at all impossible that still others exist. We are informed that the word was in use before the discovery of America, to designate an island, whose situation is not revealed, where navigators were in the habit of gathering wood for dyeing purposes,[1] and that after the discovery of South America, this same species of tree was found on the banks of the Amazon. But that does not account for the transferrence of the name to such remote parts as the Arctic or Antarctic regions, where there is no probability that the same kind of trees flourished. " Wieser finds the name Brazil, as applied to Cabral's *Sancta Cruz,* in use ever after 1504," citing as the earliest instance the "terra nova de Prisilli" of the " *Beschreibung der Meerfahrt von Lissabon nach Calacut* " of that year, published in the *Jahresberichte* of the " Kreisverein für Schwaben und Neuberg (Augsburg, 1861), p. 160." Winsor, VIII, 375, note 5, where he cities also a work on *Presilly Landt.*

The earliest map on which we have seen the name is that of the Ptolemy edition of 1508, where " R. de Brasil " designates a river flowing into the Atlantic Ocean not far south of "Cap. Ste. Crucis." According to Kohl the earliest date at which it can be definitely stated that the name was usual, is 1511, from which time the name given this region by Cabral, Land of the Holy or True Cross, gradually became obsolete. On the Ptolemy map of 1513 the name occurs twice, but with differ-

---

[1] J. G. Kohl, Die beiden ältesten General-Karten von Amerika, p. 145.

ent spelling. At 23 degrees of south latitude, the " rio de brazil " flows into " porto seguro ; " and not far east of the Gulf of Darien, there is found an " y. do brassil." Reisch, in 1515, extends the name to the whole continent of South America, which he entitles " Paria seu Prisilia." The Frankfort globe, which is supposed to have been made sometime within the five years following, transfers the name to a large Antarctic continent, and calls it " Brasilia Regio ; " while the Schoener globe varies this again by calling the Antarctic continent " Brasilia inferior," and placing a " Rio de Brasil" far in the south, emptying into the Atlantic at a point south of a great stream which is evidently the Plata, but which he calls " Rio de Mezo." As in other respects we have found the annoymous official map of 1527 so good, so in this case, it confines itself to the known, and entitles the northeastern portion of the South American continent " El Brasil." So also on that of Ribero, two years later, the name is found in the right place, although somewhat lengthened, in the form "Tierra del Brasil." But the name had not yet become constant, for on the very next map, that of the British Museum, of about 1530, there is no name for the district now known as Brazil, but a river of 30 degrees south bears the name " brasilia." Grynaeus, on his map of 1531, draws a large Antarctic continent, and places on it the legend " *Terra Australis recenter inventer, sed non diem plene cognita,*" and gives this southern land the name of " Brasielie Regio." The Venitian map of 1534 has ' Brasil ' in the right place, while the one next in chronological order, the Agnese map of 1536 gives us " brazill " out in the ocean, south of " pernambucho." Of even date is probably the Oxford map, which designates apparently the whole of the southern part of South America by the name " BRAZILI," extending on both sides of the " rio de la platta ; " and in the interior of the northern portion of the continent is the name " brazile ; " but as to what the latter applies, can only be matter of supposition. Three times is the name repeated on the Lyons edition of

Ptolemy of 1541 ; once in connection with two small islands
not far west of "Anglia" (England), where the name is spelled
" brazil ;" again, designating a small river of north-eastern
South America, with the same spelling ; and finally, not far
from the Isthmus of Darien, where is located "Insula do
brassil." Homem's map of the world, which dates from the
same decade, shows a country correctly situated, with the name
" Brazil," and on the coast, at about fifteen degrees south, is a
town of " brazill." The Nancy globe, of the middle of the
sixteenth century, calls the southern part of the continent
" Bresilia Regio," and the territory usually known by that
name, receives here the appellation " Papagalli tera." On the
Bellero map of 1554, " Bresilia " is confined to a comparatively
small district in the northeast corner of the continent, by the
undue extension of " Andaluzia nova," and the province contains a ' R. del brasil ;' but a more considerable peculiarity is
presented by the famous Ramusio map of 1556 on which the
name " Brasil " is duplicated ; once for the whole eastern part
of South America, its western border being the " Rio Maragnon," which flows from " Chili " due north, thus dividing the
continent into two nearly equal portions ; and Ramusio calls
the whole southern continent of the New World " *la parte,*
che si chiama la terra del Brasil & Peru " (the part which is
called the land of Brazil and Peru). Not satisfied with this,
he gives us a second " Brasil " as a small island between
" Irlanda " and the Isle of " Man " ! Two maps of 1560 are
preserved to us, one by Dolfinatto, on which " brasil " is a
little island at about 60 degrees north, somewhat east of
" Tiera de Bacalos," and the other by Furlani, on which an
island bearing the same name finds place near the 65th parallel,
close to " Tierra de Laborador." Still another place was found
for this poor wandering child of fancy, by Zaltieri, (1566) who
designates a diminutive island southeast of the Gulf of St.
Lawrence by that name. Ortelius (1570) has the ' R. de
Brasil," so often encountered on the eastern coast, near the
twentieth parallel, south, and says also, apparently in reference
6

to the country: *"Brasilia a Lusitanis A°. 1504 inventa."* Lok's map in the Hakluyt edition of 1582 has "Brasil" as a small island on the first meridian, which is probably that of the Cape Verde Islands. The island is about 50 degrees north, and somewhat southwest of "Hibernia;" in the edition of 1589 the island is about the same, while the continental territory, generally known under that name, is curiously called "Humos Brasi." The Judaeus map of the same year places near together "Brasil" and "S. Branda," another mythical island that remained on the maps till a comparatively late period, and both somewhat east of "Nova Francia." Then we have four maps which approach the normal much more nearly, as they all bear "Brasilia" in the northeastern part of South America, with greater or less extent. These are the maps of Myrtius of 1587, of Hondius of 1589, of Plancius, 1594, and of Hakluyt's edition of 1598. To these may be added also the work of Martines of Messina, of 1578, with the abridged form of the name 'brasil.' However, in 1598 appeared the so-called map of Porro, whereon "Brasil" again indicates mythical islands, situated not far from and to the southwest of "Hibernia." Thus ends the sixteenth century; and with the opening of the seventeenth, the name is firmly fixed as the designation of the northeastern part of South America. The boundaries of the country so known were however still undefined, and in fact remained so when, in the early part of the present century, universal revolutions shook the whole continent, and resulted in all but a diminutive portion of it being declared free from the further rule of Europe; and the people themselves were called upon to settle their mutual borders. One thing however is worthy of remark, namely that the method of spelling the name which remained the favorite one throughout the sixteenth century, that is with an *s*, has now generally given way to the modern form with *z*.

Canada.

The history of this geographical name is another illustration of the growth of the local to the general; for, going back to the time of Cartier, in the first half of the sixteenth century, we find it applied to a hamlet on or near the banks of the St. Lawrence. Whether the term was generic in its application to any small collection of houses is not clear to my mind; for though we have a statement to that effect, by one author, it is denied by another, who applies it to a fixed district; and the maps may be interpreted in accordance with either theory. As we shall see, a special town of that name is put down on quite a number of maps in very much the same place, and on other maps the name is evidently applied to a district of greater or less area. Regarding the ultimate origin of the name, there is some room for doubt; for though the early explorers evidently took it for an indigenous word, modern philological investigation points to another conclusion. Professor A. M. Elliott, after examining the word with reference to other Indian words of this section says :[1]—" According to mere form then, irrespective of the positive and forcible considerations that tend to fix a totally different etymon for the geographical term Canada, we may eliminate the present favorite Indian etymology from our discussion." Turning, then, to the European languages, he finds the word in use as a common noun in both Spanish and Portuguese; and either alone or in combination, often employed in the designation of topographical sites. Seeking analogies in the use of the words Florida and Barbada as adjectives limiting *terra*, he would interpret Canada in the same manner. " The origin of the root *can* is, of course, the Latin *canna* a reed, which gives regularly in Spanish Cañ-ada, the common term for " glade." In modern Portuguese, can-ada denotes 1, a measure for liquids, of little more than a liter ; 2, a path." The Spanish

---

pronunciation, however, is Cañáda, which must be changed in order to adapt it to the laws of English pronunciation. " In form, then, *canada* follows the Portuguese rule; in signification, the Spanish derivative from the Latin canna." " But it is probable that we have here a simple non-palatalized product for Latin *nn* such as belonged to the older period of the Spanish language." The name is found more than fifty times in Spain to-day, and survives in the Argentine Republic, for the designation of low districts not unlike those on the St. Lawrence. The name occurs too in France as a geographical term ; and our author is of the opinion that if the history of any one of the seven French places bearing it, can be traced back to a time preceding the beginning of the sixteenth century, that that would be proof conclusive of the European origin of the word. Cartier's " *Recit* " has been carefully read to arrive at the meaning he himself attached to the word, and Professor Elliott comes to the conclusion that " There cannot be the slightest doubt after these divers statements, intended to represent so varied events, and widely separated, too, in point of time, that the only use to which the name was then applied, was simply to indicate a limited district of country lying along the north bank of the St. Lawrence between the Saguenay and Quebec." " The fact, then, I hold to be incontestable that CARTIER found the name Canada already in existence as applied to a single province when he arrived at Stadacona (Quebec) in the month of September 1535." Far be it from us to dispute Professor Elliott's philology ; but he stops short of satisfying our curiosity, by not explaining how a Spanish word came to be in common use among a tribe of savages who had seen practically nothing of the Spaniards. The Spaniards were theoretically acquainted with the Canadian coast from an early period, as we see by the official maps of 1527 and 1529; but that they were at all familiar with the interior of the country, along the banks of the St. Lawrence, we have seen no proof; and would be disposed to doubt it until shown good reason to the contrary. That they ever remained here long enough to make an impression on the Indian mind, is still more questionable. Furthermore, when it is considered how difficult it is to root out an old geographical name and substitute a new one, especially among people of low intelligence, and little accustomed to change, it seems to us very improbable that a visit or two from Spanish navigators, even if they ever penetrated so far up the St. Lawrence, would be sufficient to revolutionize the native name of a district. Mr. Marcou's theory as to the derivation of the name America from the fact of Columbus and his followers having heard the word Americ from the lips of the savages as the designation of the source of their gold supplies, is called " foolish " by Mr. H. H. Bancroft; yet we have frequent analogy of the adoption of the Indian name by explorers; can Mr. Elliott show us any analogous adoptions by the American Indians of European words as the names of their territories? If so, we might see more probability in his etymology. Moreover, if the Spaniards had used this term to designate the country on the St. Lawrence, would we not find it on at least one or the other of their early maps? So far as my investigations go, I have failed to find it there.

The earliest map on which I have noticed the name Canada is that of Vallard, No. 155 of the Kohl Collection. It is there used to designate a small district on the north bank of the St. Lawrence, between an unnamed island (Orleans?) and a lake to the west which is called simply " le lac." On an anonymous map, which Kohl supposes to be from the year 1548 or thereabouts, the name Canada occurs three times; namely, once in large letters, between the Gulf of St. Lawrence and the " Mer de France ;" again it is seen in small letters east of the " R. du Sagnay," and north of the St. Lawrence River ; and a third time it finds a place southwest of the given portion of the river St. Lawrence. Another anonymous French map of probably a few years later, gives apparently the name of the whole country as CANADA, in large capitals ; then the accustomed district in small capitals ; and lastly, an affluent of the

St. Lawrence, coming from the north, bears the same name. Diego Homem, on his map of 1558, uses the name for an island situated between a great river, evidently the St. Lawrence, on the south, and " Mare leparaniatiñ " on the north. On a map of 1556 by Sanson d'Abbeville, " Le Canada " is the designation of a large territory, extending from a line south of the St. Lawrence River and the mountains of " Virginie " to a line in the north, separating it from " Estotilande ou Terre de Labrador " and " Nouvelle Bretagne." This map introduces us also to an appellation of the St. Lawrence River which held ground for a time but apparently never became popular : " La Gr. Riv. de Canada ou de St. Laurens." This magnificent stream remained for a long time without any fixed name : here we see the transition stage, giving a choice of names ; but in the end the saint's name crowded out the native one, probably because the latter would ever have necessitated the joining of some explicative adjective with it, as in this case " Grande." A map of this region by Guitierrez, of the year 1562 contains " Canada Prov." north of " Tierre Francisca " and of " Tierra di Norimberga." Ortelius (1570) calls the whole district west of the " Saguenai fl." by the name CANADA, and names a town in the southern part of the province, and near the St. Lawrence River " Canado." On Thevet's map, extracted from the work " La France Antarctic," " Canade " is a town situated on a small river entering the St. Lawrence from the north. Sir Humphrey Gilbert had still another idea of the application of this name ; for on the map in his " Discourse," " Canada " is a large island east of " La nuova Franza." Martines' map in the British Museum places the province of " Canada " west of " Baccilaos." On Hakluyt's map contained in the edition of 1589, " Canada " is a town of " Nova Francia." Frobisher makes of Canada a peninsula, occupying the northeastern portion of North America between " bacalaos " and " Hispania nova." In the title of his map of 1593, Judaeus mentions Canada as one of the principal divisions of North America, and twice in notes speaks of the natives under the name "Canadenses." One of these legends is at seventy degrees of north latitude, and reads: "*Hoc mare dulcium aquarum est, cujus terminus ignorari Canadenses aijunt.*" The other is in southwestern California, and reads as follows: "*Qui inter Florida et Baccalaos habitant, hi omnes uno nomine Canadenses appellantur Hochelaga, Hongueda Corterealis.*" Furthermore the name Canada stands on the map for the region bounded by the St. Lawrence and the "Saguenai," Hochelaga and Hongueda. Whytfliet's map of the country, issued in 1597 is entitled "Nova Francia et Canada," and Canada in capital letters is placed in the north, and again in small letters is used to designate a town on a branch of the St. Lawrence, not far from the main stream. Lescarbot's map of 1609 multiplies the name in a manner to indicate his fondness for it. Thus we have the "Golfe de Canada," "La grande R. de Canada," besides two districts bearing the name; one immediately south of the mouth of the St. Lawrence River, and the other west of the "R. de Saguenay." If this map were seventy-five or one hundred years older than it is, we should feel inclined to accept Professor Elliott's interpretation of the origin of the name: for it looks very much like a generic term applied to various localities which it describes, without taking the trouble to specify more exactly by the use of individual proper names. On No. 167 of Kohl's Collection, which he gives as a copy of Purchas' map of 1625, "New France" is the name of the great stretch of country north of the St. Lawrence, while the Gulf and River of St. Lawrence are named respectively "Golfe of Canada" and "The great riuer of Canada." De Laet's map of 1630 gives "La Grand Riviere de Canada" but calls the gulf "S. Laurens." A district north of the "Baye de Chaleur" bears the legend "Canadiens." We have thus examined the maps of a century following the first introduction of the geographical name Canada, as far as we have been able to find them. The name was by no means universally adopted in the earlier days; and it is safe to say that the majority of maps of this period which have come under our notice employ the French official name for the country, that is New France. The shorter and more easily pronounced word crowded out of use the longer name; and survived even the British conquest, which the name New France could scarcely have done. What will be the result if Canada is ever incorporated in the United States, we leave for the future to decide.

V.

Development of American National and State Boundaries.

Before the era of Columbus the vast space between Europe on the east and Asia on the west, was practically a blank in the consciousness of the civilized world. From his voyage in 1492 may be reckoned the birth of the western continent; which, in the subsequent period of exploration, gradually rose as it were piece by piece out of the ocean, and assumed visible form and shape to the eye of observing Europe. But long before the whole was known, the secondary development began, with the acquisition of more detailed knowledge of the immediate surroundings of the several colonies. As in organic bodies, the internal development continues after the outer form is fixed, so with our geographical development, the internal organs of states and countries have been slowly developing toward fixity after the outer form had been definitely settled. At the same time, the claims of jurisdiction have gone through numerous changes, the principal being the gradual narrowing of pretensions to universal dominion over newly discovered territory, to a claim of that district actually in possession. The first charter of Columbus conferred on him the admiralty of such "Islands and Continent" as he might discover.[1] On his return, Spain, wishing to obtain the monopoly of all lands that might be discovered in that direction, applied to the pope for a confirmation of her title. This

---

[1] *Charters and Constitutions*, compiled by Ben. Perley Poore, I, 304.

resulted in the famous bulls of Pope Alexander VI, by which all non-Christian unknown lands of the earth were divided between Spain and Portugal, by a line extending north and south, from pole to pole, and passing one hundred leagues west of the Azores and Cape Verde Islands. Portugal protested so strongly against this arrangement that she forced Spain to a treaty by which that line was moved two hundred and seventy leagues toward the west. Resting on this grant of the pope, Spain claimed universal jurisdiction in the New World, with the exception of a portion of South America, which, by the above mentioned treaty of Tordesillas, fell to the Portuguese. The other marine powers were unwilling that Spain should monopolize the vast unknown possibilities of the New World, and followed in her footsteps in sending out exploring expeditions. Later came the period of settlement, which, with the English, and therefore the most important for the history of the United States, may be considered to have commenced with Raleigh's charter of March 25, 1584, by which he received from the English crown, for himself, his heirs and assigns, " free libertie and licence from time to time, and at all times for euer hereafter, to discouer, search, finde out, and view such remote, heathen and barbarous lands, countreis, and territories not actually possessed of any Christian Prince, nor inhabited by Christian People, as to him, his heirs and assigns, and to euery or any of them shall seeme good." He was to have the fee-simple of all lands discovered, and the rights of government over all " that shall abide within 200. leagues of any of the saide place or places, where the said Walter Ralegh . . . shall inhabite within 6. yeeres next ensuing the date hereof."

In the grant of 1606 to the Virginia Company, the more definite limits of from thirty-four to forty-five degrees of north latitude in America were assigned. Later by the charter of Carolina, issued in 1665, territory so far south as the twenty-ninth degree of north latitude was granted, notwithstanding the fact that the Spaniards had first explored this region, and that a Spanish colony of nearly or quite a century's existence was within the territory now granted. Under such circumstances conflicts were sure to arise. France had also some show of claim to this territory on account of her early settlement at Port Royal. But she preferred in the end, to apply her energies further north, where her claims came in conflict with those of England. The Dutch, who were enterprising mariners also, did not fail to set up a claim to a portion of the New World, both on the ground of discovery and of first settlement; and even the Swedes, in their period of prosperity, essayed to establish by colonization a claim to territory on this side the Atlantic. How were all these conflicting interests to be reconciled? It was a new experiment in the world's history; and only time could solve the difficult problem here presented. Portugal's right to unexplored lands, granted by a bull of Pope Eugene IV. had been acquiesced in by other nations,[1] probably because the prize did not seem worth contending for. But the hope of finding gold in America, combined with the change of ideas wrought by the Reformation, presented too strong a temptation for the nations of western Europe to resist. International law, itself then a new science, was not of sufficient influence to enforce a policy according to its principles. Abstract ideas of justice seldom if ever prevail in such cases, where self-interest gets the upper hand. Hence we find that the old rule of might makes right was the guiding principle by which America became divided among its present owners.

The ease with which these vast stretches of land were given away on paper, led to a lavishness and carelessness in their disposal, even among the subjects of the same power, which finally produced endless trouble. We have seen the extensive and indefinite nature of Raleigh's grant. Under it no permanent settlement was formed. Then came the grant of 1606, dividing the whole territory from 34° to 45° north latitude

---

[1] W. Robertson, *Hist. of America.* 3 vols. Basil, 1790, v. I, p. 58.

between two branches of the same company, but leaving the district between the 38th and 41st degrees open to both; forbidding, however, each to found a settlement within one hundred miles of the other. In 1609 there was granted to the London Company the territory extending 200 miles north and 200 miles south of Point Comfort, with the islands within 100 miles of the coast, while the grant of the mainland was to extend "from the Sea Coast of the Precinct aforesaid, up into the Land throughout from Sea to Sea, West and Northwest." A glance at the map shows that this grant includes the coast-line of a part of New Jersey, all of Delaware, Maryland and North Carolina, to say nothing of the vast interior stretching to the Pacific. The present State of Virginia is, in extent of territory, the mere shadow of the magnificent domain granted under that name in 1609. The first important reduction came through the grant of Maryland in 1632. The Virginians protested against this cutting off "nere two-third parts of the better territory of Virginia," but without effect. The same rule of the right of might held good here, as it did between the different nations; the Virginia Company had been deprived of their governmental powers, though their property rights were guaranteed them. Lord Baltimore was the stronger at court and retained what had been granted him. Carolina was later cut off from the other side; and so the mutilation continued.

The case was similar in the north. To the "second Collony" was granted in 1620 the region between the fortieth and forty-eighth parallels of latitude, and extending to the Pacific. Out of this tract were afterward carved, by the government and by the company, so many grants that it was almost impossible to bring order out of the resulting chaos.

What then were the causes that led to this confusion, sowed the seeds of discord among the colonists themselves and also among the respective European countries? First and foremost were the extravagant pretensions of the different courts in claiming immense regions of which they were not able to take possession. In this respect England took the lead; for though her charters almost invariably granted only such lands as were not already owned or occupied by any Christian prince or People, she herself and her colonists gave practically no heed to this clause, and. in several instances drove out or subdued others, who by every principle of justice were better entitled to the soil than their conquerors. A second reason was the carelessness with which grants were made; the king, though he never dies, seeming to have had a very poor memory as to past actions, as soon as he wished, in an easy and cheap manner, to reward a new favorite. But the trouble was brought about as much by ignorance as by carelessness;—reliance on the descriptions of travelers, and on crude and imperfect maps, being a very potent cause. The art of map-making was not yet well developed. Furthermore the astronomers had not then succeeded in determining accurately the latitude and longitude of even the main cities of Europe; while the instruments for observations at sea were still more crude and inaccurate than those employed on land. Measurements of portions of the earth had indeed been essayed, to establish the length of a degree of latitude; but it was after the middle of the seventeenth century [1669] before an approach to accurateness was reached in France; and so slow was the spread of scientific knowledge in those times, that it took ten years for the knowledge of the French measurements to find its way to the Royal Society of London. The early English settlements to the south of the 40th parallel were so far from the Spaniards that the latter, though theoretically claiming the entire continent, did not attempt to disturb them. It was otherwise however with the northern colonies. France and England were both deeply interested in the fisheries, and both wished to obtain possession of the neighboring lands. In the seventeenth century the principal territory in dispute was the eastern coast of Maine. As early as December 18th, 1603, King Henry IV. of France had granted to Sieur de Monts the country from the 40th to the

46th degree of north latitude. In the following year this enterprising Frenchman had a settlement on what is now the coast of Nova Scotia; and with this as a central point, he claimed the neighboring territory according to the terms of his patent. The first English patent covering this territory in definite terms was that of 1606, which however for this region remained practically a dead letter till after the settlement of Plymouth in 1620. In this year the "second Collony" received the charter for "New England in America," limited on the north by the 48th parallel of latitude. Settlements increased rapidly; and it was not long before the representatives of the two nations found their interests clashing. The French finally narrowed their claims and expressed a willingness to consider Pemaquid Point, which was about half way between the Penobscot and Kennebec rivers, as their western limit. In as much as the French settlements were much the earlier, this establishing a middle point as mutual boundary was, in theory at least, a cession on their part; and according to modern ideas of international law, would have been eminently just. But England, who ever denied Spain's right to possession as against herself, on the score of mere discovery, was strenuous in asserting her own rights, which had no better basis, as against France. As the English colonists were the more numerous, they finally succeeded in obtaining by force of arms that which no modern court of justice or international tribunal would have awarded them. At the treaty of Utrecht, (1713) France was forced to cede to England " Acadia and Nova Scotia, with its ancient boundaries." A half century passes, of bickerings, mutual recriminations and wars; and again France is forced to acknowledge herself conquered, and cedes to England " Canada with all its dependencies also the Island of Cape Breton, and all other islands and coasts in the gulf and river of St. Lawrence, and generally all that belongs to the said country, lands, islands and coasts." At the same time England surrenders her claims to the territory west to the Pacific and accepts the Mississippi as her western border.

To the south of the English colonies was Spanish Florida, under which name the Spaniards claimed an indefinite extent of territory northwards. However, the English did not hesitate to claim this country also, and grant charters for the same. Although the actual settlements of South Carolina did not extend to an uncomfortable proximity to the Spaniards, constant unrest and occasional war between the representatives of the two nations, disturbed both colonies. In 1732 Georgia was chartered, with southern limits bounded by the Altamaha River. War again broke out, with varying fortunes for the contestants. But as the English succeeded in maintaining their post at the mouth of the St. Mary's, that river, instead of the Altamaha, ultimately became the southern boundary of Georgia. By the treaty of Paris [1763], Spain ceded Florida to England in exchange for Cuba; and France ceded to Spain by a separate treaty, Louisiana west of the Mississippi, together with the island of New Orleans.

Such was the condition of the boundaries when the struggle broke out that ended in the establishment of American independence. According to the definitive treaty of peace, signed at Paris September 3, 1783, between England and the United States, the boundaries of the latter were fixed as follows :—
" From the North-West angle of Nova Scotia, viz. that angle which is formed by a line drawn due north, from the source of Saint-Croix river to the Highlands which divide those rivers that empty themselves into the river St. Lawrence, from those which fall into the Atlantic Ocean, to the north western-most head of Connecticut river; thence down along the middle of that river to the forty-fifth degree of north-latitude; from thence by a line due west on said latitude until it strikes the river Iroquois or Catarquy ; thence along the middle of the said river into lake Ontario, through the middle of said lake, until it strikes the communication by water between that lake and lake Erie ; thence along the middle of said communication into lake Erie through the middle of said lake until it arrives at the water communication between that lake and

lake Huron; thence along the middle of said water communication into the lake Huron; thence through the middle of said lake to the water communication between that lake and lake Superior; thence through lake Superior, northward of the isles Royal and Philipeaux, to the Long-Lake and the water communication between it and the lake of the Woods; thence through the said lake to the most north-western point thereof, and from thence on a due west course to the river Mississippi; thence by a line to be drawn along the middle of the said river Mississippi until it shall intersect the northernmost part of the thirty-first degree of north latitude;— South, by a line to be drawn due east from the determination of the line last mentioned, in the latitude of thirty-one degrees north of the Equator, to the middle of the river Apalachicola or Catahouche; thence along the middle thereof to its junction with the Flint river; thence straight to the head of St. Mary's river, and thence down along the middle of St. Mary's river to the Atlantic Ocean :—East, by a line to be drawn along the middle of the river St. Croix, from its mouth in the bay of Fundy to its source; and from its source directly north to the aforesaid Highlands, which divide the rivers that fall into the Atlantic Ocean from those which fall into the river St. Lawrence; comprehending all islands within twenty leagues of any part of the shores of the United States, and lying between lines to be drawn due east from the points where the aforesaid boundaries between Nova Scotia on the one part, and East Florida on the other, shall respectively touch the bay of Fundy, and the Atlantic Ocean; excepting such islands as now are, or heretofore have been, within the limits of the said province of Nova Scotia."[1]

Spain returned the province of Louisiana to France by the treaty of St. Ildefonso, October 1st, 1800, " with the same extent as it now has in the hands of Spain, and as it had when France possessed it, and as it should be according to the "

---

[1] Martens et Cussy, *Recueil de traités*, I, 312.

treaties subsequently made between Spain and other states."
By the treaty signed at Paris, April 30th, 1803, Napoleon
ceded to the United States, in the name of the French Republic, Louisiana, " forever and in full sovereignty, . . . with all
its rights and appurtenances, thus and in the manner that it
was acquired by the French Republic, in virtue of the above-
mentioned treaty, concluded with His Catholic Majesty."[1]
The borders between Louisiana and the Spanish provinces on
the west and south had never been defined. The United
States having purchased the former, were disposed to extend
their claim as far as possible. "The French had ever regarded
the mouth of the Del Norte as the western limit of Louisiana
on the Gulf of Mexico; and the United States naturally
claimed to the same point."[2] But the Spaniards were not by
any means disposed to cede so much territory; and the result,
instead of a war, as it would have been at an earlier period,
was a long series of negotiations, with a peaceable settlement
finally of the difficulties. Spain claimed, in right of her settlement at Santa Fe, the territory to the Mississippi; and
furthermore insisted that she had ceded to France in 1800 the
Spanish not the French territory of Louisiana. As there was
no pressing need of settlement and each party refused to recede
from its demands, the matter was allowed to rest, until the
circumstances had changed and each was more disposed to
make concessions for the sake of peace. This change was
brought about by a dispute between the same powers concerning Florida. Both divisions of the latter province had been
retroceded by England to Spain in 1783; the same boundaries
as are fixed by the treaty of 1783 with England are ratified
by a treaty between the United States and Spain in 1795.
However in 1810, the United States seize the greater part of
West Florida, to keep it from falling into the hands of the
British, from whom trouble is expected, and who are consequently not wanted as a neighbor on the south as well as on

---

[1] *Ibid.*, II, 283. [2] T. Twiss, *The Oregon Question*, p. 230.

7

the north. In the later discussions as to boundaries, Spain waives "all demands on this head;" and after many propositions and counter-propositions, an arrangement satisfactory to both parties was finally reached, which was embodied in the provisions of the treaty of Washington, February 22d, 1819. In accordance therewith Spain yielded both the Floridas to the United States, while the latter resigned their claim to Texas and agreed to pay to their own citizens claims to the amount of $5,000,000 which the latter had against Spain. Between Louisiana and Mexico, the boundaries were agreed upon as follows:— "The boundary-line between the two countries, west of the Mississippi, shall begin on the Gulph of Mexico, at the mouth of the river Sabine, in the sea, continuing north, along the western bank of that River, to the 32d degree of latitude; thence, by a line due north, to the degree of latitude where it strikes the Rio Roxo of Nachitoches, or Red River; then following the course of the Rio Roxo westward, to the degree of longitude 100 west from London and 23 from Washington; then, crossing the said Red River, and running thence, by a line due north, to the river Arkansas; thence, following the course of the southern bank of the Arkansas, to its source, in latitude 42 north; and thence, by that parallel of latitude, to the South Sea;"[1] the United States to have all the islands in the rivers; but the navigation to be free to both nations. The purchase of Louisiana from France gave to the United States their first claim to territory west of the Mississippi River; and in the course of these negotiations with Spain, had appeared for the first time, a claim on their part to the region west to the Pacific.[2] It was not long till this claim assumed definite proportions in respect to lands farther north than the boundaries now established with Spain; and it was to require all the learning and statesmanship of the young republic to establish international recognition to those claims.

[1] Martens et Cussy, III, 410, *et seq.*　　　[2] Twiss, p. 238.

As far as Spain was concerned, the United States were now at liberty to lay claim to the entire western part of North America north of the forty-second parallel. But therein they came at once in contact, if not in conflict, with the claims of other powers. Although Spain had at one time claimed exclusive jurisdiction to the entire western coast of North America as far north as the sixtieth degree, England had not only not respected Spain's assumed rights, but had finally compelled her, when in difficulty, to sign the convention of the Escurial, October 28, 1790, by which both parties "agreed that their respective subjects shall not be disturbed or molested, either in navigating or carrying on their fisheries in the Pacific Ocean, or in the South Seas, or in landing on the coasts of those seas, in places not already occupied, for the purpose of carrying on their commerce with the natives of the country, or of making settlements there; the whole subject, nevertheless, to the restrictions and provisions specified in the three following articles:"[1] These articles provided (1) that Spain should have exclusive jurisdiction over a territory of ten sea leagues radius from any of her existing settlements; (2) that all settlements made since April, 1789, or to be made thereafter, should be free of access to the trade of both nations; (3) that neither party should thereafter make settlements in South America at any place south of the existing Spanish settlements. From the time of this treaty, England maintained that she had all the rights of settlement and commerce in common with Spain, in the region north of the 38th parallel, the position of the most northerly of Spain's then existing settlements on the Pacific coast; and she accordingly denied that the United States, by the treaty of ·1819, could have any higher right than Spain had had. But there was still another party who claimed an interest in this territory. In Russia, which had at an early period established hunting and trading stations far to the north-west, there was issued on the 16th of

[1] *Ibid.*, 113, *et seq.*

September, 1821, an imperial ukase asserting exclusive jurisdiction over "the north-west coast of America, as far south as
51° north lat.," and prohibiting "all foreign vessels from approaching within one hundred miles of the shore, under
penalty of confiscation."[1] Both the United States and England protested against this assumption of territorial jurisdiction by Russia; and, by the conventions of 1824 and 1825
respectively, they succeeded in having Russia resign all claims
south of 54° 40' north latitude. Thus the contest was narrowed down to the two representatives of the Anglo-Saxon
race; and long and determinedly, though without war, they
wrestled for the jurisdiction. The apple of discord was the
basin of the Columbia River, to which England claimed at
least an equal right with the United States; and proposed to
have that river as their mutual boundary, with the navigation
free to both; but the United States would be satisfied with
nothing less than exclusive possession of the whole.

The treaty of 1783 had provided that the boundary between
the United States and the British posessions of the northwest
should be a due west course from the Lake of the Woods to
the Mississippi. By 1794 it had become doubtful if the
Mississippi extended so far north; and the treaty of Ghent
(1814) settled the matter by fixing the forty-ninth parallel as
the mutual boundary. By the convention of 1818 this boundary was extended to the "Stony" (Rocky) Mountains; and
the territory beyond was to be open to both parties.

The disputed part of the Pacific coast had been visited from
time to time by Spanish, English, and Russian ships; but not
one of them had entered the mouth of the Columbia River,
before Captain Gray, in 1789, in an American trading ship,
made his way over the bar that obstructs the entrance and
sailed for some distance up the stream. In 1803, "Mr. Jefferson, then President of the United States, commissioned
Captains Lewis and Clarke to explore the River Missouri and"

---

[1] *Ibid.*, 254.

" its principal branches to their sources, and then to seek and trace to its termination in the Pacific some stream, whether the Columbia, the Oregon, the Colorado, or any other, which might offer the most direct and practicable water communication across the continent for the purposes of commerce." [1] They found and explored the Columbia, from one of its sources to its mouth. Relying on these grounds of discovery and on the fact that an American company made the first settlement in the district, the United States laid claim to the whole basin of the Columbia; and after the treaty of 1819 with Spain, considered their title as unimpeachable, in as much as Spanish mariners had been the first to make nearer observations of the coast. England insisted on the right of occupation in common, urging the convention of 1790 with Spain as a recognition of that right. Our government first claimed to the 51st parallel, as lying within the basin of the Columbia; but later offered as a compromise, to extend to the Pacific the already existing boundary-line which divided the territories of the two nations, as far as the Rocky Mountains, namely, the 49th parallel. For a long time England would not listen to this, always insisting that the navigation of the Columbia was necessary to the prosperity of her northwest territory. The matter was finally compromised and settled by the Oregon treaty of 1846, by which free navigation of the river was guaranteed to the Hudson's Bay Company and those trading with it. The boundary-line was to be the 49th parallel to the end of the mainland, thence through the Georgia and Juan de Fuca straits to the Pacific. The discoveries, explorations, and first settlement of the Americans in this region, should have given them some advantage, on the principle now recognized by the Powers, in reference to Africa; but the best ground for the justice of this method of settlement seems to be the fact that possession in common, by two nations, of the whole country from the 42d degree to 54° 40' was not practicable; and as neither had

---

[1] *Ibid.,* 14–15.

exclusive rights, from discovery or settlement on the Pacific coast, but practically, if not theoretically, claimed the district as an extension of that already in possession, it was the most natural course to extend to the Pacific the dividing line which was already in existence east of the Rocky Mountains.

There was to be still another enlargement of territory before the United States should receive the form which now appears so symmetrical and natural on the map. By the treaty of 1819 they had surrendered all claim to the district between the boundary then fixed—Sabine and Arkansas Rivers—and the Rio Grande del Norte. However, this region became peopled with a large proportion of English-speaking immigrants, who were discontented with the government as a member of the Mexican States, which had been independent of Spain since 1821. They accordingly declared their independence from Mexico; and from 1837 to 1845 remained an independent republic. In the latter year the country was admitted, at her own request, to the American Union as one of the states. The dissatisfaction of Mexico at this step led to a war, the result of which was that the United States took not only Texas, but the whole district west to the Pacific and south to the junction of the Colorado and Gila rivers. But not yet was the desire for more satisfied; for it was found that there were lacking good routes of communication between the eastern and western parts of the newly-acquired territory; and hence our government had to go again to Mexico, this time with gold instead of arms in her hand, and ask for a strip south of the Gila River, which was bought for $10,000,000, and is known under the name of the Gadsden purchase.[1]

Having thus followed in short the widening of the English borders in North America, till that nation possessed almost all to the east of the Mississippi; then the establishment of an

---

[1] As Alaska is distant and separated from the rest of the United States, it is not deemed necessary here to enter into the matter of the purchase in 1867, from Russia, of this tract of more than 500,000 square miles.

independent state of the same people, in the New World, and
the enlargement of this state through purchase and conquest,
until it became about three times its original size, we turn our
attention to the development of the interior lines of demarcation. This is a study of no less importance, and in some respects of greater interest, than the other. We have already
seen how England from the first claimed ownership of the
entire central belt of the continent, and gave to one company,
divided into two sections, the right to take possession of, people,
and govern this immense territory. The task proved too great
for the company; then, too, there were others ready and
anxious to undertake the work of colonization; and they
asked for, and received permission to found colonies within
the bounds already prescribed, but generally with the condition attached that lands so granted were not already occupied
by Christian people. The first reduction of Virginia's territory was made in favor of Lord Baltimore, a court favorite
who had already attempted to plant a colony in the southeastern part of Newfoundland, and failed. Admiring the
country and climate of Virginia, he secured a grant of the
territory north and east of the Potomac River and extending
to the 40th parallel of north latitude. He dying before the
charter was sealed, a new instrument was drawn up in favor
of his son Cecil, second Lord Baltimore. Previous to this,
the government of Virginia had been taken out of the hands
of the company, though the judgment on the process of *quo
warranto* had never been formally entered till Baltimore applied for the patent. Furthermore, the possessory rights of
the company had been frequently assured to them. The early
days of the colony had not been prosperous ones for its founders and financial backers. Now that the colony was firmly
established and there was a prospect of reaping rich returns
on the original outlay, the members of the company regarded
this grant to Baltimore as a serious infringement on their
rights, and complained loudly thereof. Those were days of
despotism; and the Virginians spoke to deaf ears. The

government received a legal decision in its favor, Lord Justice Holt deciding that "the laws of England do not extend to Virginia ; being a conquered country, their law is what the King pleases."[1] So Lord Baltimore retained his grant and planted his colony. The day was to come, however, when the tables would be turned ; and his descendants would hear a somewhat similar judgment, but this time against them ; and after long delay, they also would have to submit.

In the meantime the Dutch had discovered, explored, and settled the region along the Hudson river; and also made some attempts to settle the Delaware valley, which, however, were at first unsuccessful. The Swedes, carrying out a cherished plan of Gustavus Adolphus, made their way to the same district, bought lands of the Indians, and commenced what, under favoring circumstances, might have grown to a large and flourishing colony. However, they failed to live in peace with their European neighbors, and fell before the greater power of the Dutch. Thus the Swedish colony became incorporated in the New Netherlands ; and Dutch settlers began to people the banks of the Delaware. To the east, the Dutch were not so fortunate. Though the first English settlements there were not so old as the Dutch trading post on the Hudson, still they were more flourishing and grew very much more rapidly. At first the Dutch were rather traders than colonists ; and when they began to realize the importance of peopling the country with an agricultural and industrial population, they introduced a system akin to feudalism which was not calculated to foster colonial growth of a healthy nature. The Dutch, having established a post on the Connecticut River, claimed the entire valley. But the English coming in numbers thither, the Dutch were compelled to allow them at first equal privileges there, and at last to yield, making a provisional treaty by which they gave up all claims to the mainland east of a point near the present city of Green-

---

[1] Hildreth, *U. S. Hist.*, II, 125.

wich, retaining on the Connecticut only their fort of Good Hope.

Under the English charter of 1606 there was no colony planted in the northern district set off by that document. The Pilgrim Fathers had planned to settle further south than they actually did ; and first obtained a patent for the lands they occupied, after they were settled in their new homes. Though they drew up a plan for self-government before they landed, they never succeeded in gaining a royal charter conferring the powers of government on them. In fact, however, they governed themselves for a long time, but could not prevent their territory finally (1691) being incorporated with Massachusetts.

On November 3, 1620, was issued the charter for " New England in America," under which name was to be included "all that Circuit, Continent, Precincts, and Limits in America, lying and being in Breadth, from Fourty Degrees of Northerly Latitude, from the Equinoctiall Line, to Fourty-eight Degrees of the said Northerly Latitude, and in length by all the Breadth aforesaid throughout the Maine Land, from Sea to Sea." This immense tract, like that of Virginia, was to be subjected to many future amputations. The Dutch claimed the territory from the fortieth to the forty-fifth parallel ; and were already, at the time of the issuing of this patent, in possession of the Hudson river country, with a settlement farther north than 42° 30'. To the north, the French were already in possession, having for many years before this time had a trading post as far south as about the 44th parallel. Accordingly, if the English had abided by the letter of their charters, they would not have claimed more than the territory between the already existing Dutch and French settlements, or less than one and a half degrees of latitude, instead of eight.

The development of the New England boundary-lines is difficult to follow. There were two granting powers, the crown and the Plymouth Company ; and their respective grants were not always in harmony ; moreover, the successive grants of each were often inconsistent with its own earlier grants. The result was confusion twice confounded. To examine all the details of the various grants would take us much beyond the limits of a lecture. We may take as a central point the grant of Massachusetts Bay; as it was not only the largest tract conveyed to any one party, but the district so ceded was soon to become the main colony of New England. On the 19th of March, 1628, the Plymouth Company conveyed to John Humphrey and others the domain ; and on the 4th of the following March, a royal charter was issued confirming the same and granting governmental powers over the tract described as follows :—"All that Parte of Newe England in America, which lyes and extendes betweene a great River there, comonlie called Monomack River, alias Merrimack River, and a certen other River there, called Charles River, being in the Bottome of a certen Bay there, comonlie called Massachusetts, alias Mattachusetts, alias Massatusetts Bay ; and also all and singuler those Landes and Hereditaments whatsoever, lying within the Space of Three Englishe Myles on the South Parte of the said River, called Charles River, or of any or every Parte thereof; and also all and singuler the Landes and Hereditaments whatsoever, lying and being within the Space of Three Englishe Myles to the south of the southernmost Parte of the said Baye, called Massachusetts, . . . Bay : And also all those Landes and Hereditaments whatsoever, which lye and be within the Space of Three Englishe Myles to the Northward of the saide River, called Monomack, alias Merrymack, or to the Northward of any and every Parte thereof, and all Landes and Hereditaments whatsoever, lying within the Lymitts aforesaide, North and South, in Latitude and Bredth, and in Length and Longitude, of and within all the Bredth aforesaide, throughout the mayne Landes there, from the Atlantick and Western Sea and Ocean on the East Parte, to the South Sea on the West Parte," including the neighboring islands.[1]   A portion of this district,

---

[1] *Char. and Cons.*, I, 194.

to the north, had already been conveyed in 1622 to Mason, and had received the name of Mariana; another portion, ten by thirty miles in extent, had been bestowed in 1623 on Robert Gorges. Massachusetts was, however, to extend her jurisdiction very considerably north and south, and then to undergo a number of amputations, before her borders should become permanently established.

That the spirit of colonization was rife in England, was not the only ground for increase in the number of distinct settlements which, in the course of a few years, sprang up in New England.[1] Grants to enterprising individuals did their work; but no less did the dissatisfaction produced by the strictness, nay harshness, of the Massachusetts authorities. To this cause in whole or in part, is due the emigration which led to the founding of the present states of Rhode Island and Connecticut. Herein lay the seeds of another conflict. Although not within her charter limits, Massachusetts laid claim to the jurisdiction over her emigrants.[2] For a time each of the off-shoots was practically independent; then gradually took place a drawing together round the two main settlements. But there was a middle district which, for more than half a century, continued to be the cause of dispute.

The Plymouth Company made at an early date, several small grants of land in the district immediately to the north of the Massachusetts Bay territory; but these were ignored and superseded by an extensive cession to John Mason, November 7th, 1629, embracing the coast from the Merrimack to the Piscataqua and sixty miles inland. As the Massachusetts Bay charter conveyed all the land to the extent of three miles north of any part of the Merrimack River, and as by

---

[1] Hildreth, I, 267, writing of the year 1640, says: "Already there existed east of the Hudson twelve independent communities, comprising not less than fifty towns or distinct settlements."

[2] *Ibid.,* I, 232. "The emigrants [of 1636] took with them a commission of government, the joint act of the Massachusetts General Court and of the commissioners representing the lords proprietors of Connecticut.

survey it was found that that river extends inland toward the northwest, Massachusetts claimed jurisdiction, and exercised it at times, over this section. After a century's dispute the matter came finally before the highest authorities in England for settlement, and Massachusetts suffered a greater diminution of territory thereby than even New Hampshire had asked or had reason to expect. "The Privy Council decided, however, that this due west line (from a point three miles north of the Merrimack River) should take its departure from a point three miles north of the southwesternmost bend of that river, thus giving to New Hampshire twenty-eight entire townships, and parts of six others settled under grants from Massachusetts."

The early history of the region now included in the state of Maine is kaleidoscopic in character; and is as little capable of short description as the complicated movements of that instrument.[1] The conflicting claims there of French and English, of Mason and Gorges, of Massachusetts, Plymouth, and New York, present an exceedingly confused picture. The English finally conquered the French in war; Massachusetts bought out Gorges' claim. After the formation of the republic, Massachusetts was induced to give up her claims, and Maine became [1820] an independent member of the Union. Its eastern boundary had been a subject of dispute between England and the United States from the time of their first treaty, —they not being able to agree as to which river was meant under the name of St. Croix. By the treaty of 1794 between these powers, a commission was constituted for determining the question. The members thereof were enabled to reach a conclusion by discovering the remains of an old fort on the banks of the stream now known as the St. Croix; and decided also that the eastern and not the western branch of the same should form the boundary. The New Hampshire line had

---

[1] *Ibid.*, I, 201. "The coast from the Piscataqua to the Kennebec was covered by six other patents [than that of Gorges], issued in the course of three years by the Council for New England."

been definitely settled by the English Privy Council at the same time [1737] as the northern line of Massachusetts had been fixed.

The royal commission of 1664 had attempted to settle boundary, as well as other disputes in New England. However, their decisions had but little permanent effect. Among other matters referred to this commission, was the settlement of the quarrel over the territory between Rhode Island and Connecticut. Orders had been given that, if it were found true, as reported, that this district had been ceded by the Indians to King Charles I, then Nicholls was to seize it in the name of the king, and give it the name of King's Province. " After hearing the parties, the commissioners directed that the territory in dispute, including the whole Narraganset country, should constitute, under the name of KING'S PROVINCE, a separate district." . . . This decision, however, did not end the matter. It was held invalid because it wanted the signature of Nicholls, whose participation was essential to all decisions of the commissioners. Disputes, both as to jurisdiction and land titles, presently revived, and were carried on for the next fifty years.* In 1683 another commission reported, " that the jurisdiction of the Narraganset country belonged to Connecticut, and the land to the Atherton Company." Rhode Island, however, charging the commissioners with partiality, succeeded in preventing the confirmation of the report. Having finally come before the king in council, the matter was settled in 1725 by giving King's Province to Rhode Island, thus confirming her charter of 1662.

The charters of Massachusetts and Connecticut had granted to those colonies an extension of their respective north and south boundaries to the Pacific Ocean. We have seen that they, especially Connecticut, came thus in conflict with the Dutch in the New Netherlands; that the latter were driven from the Connecticut river, with the exception of the land occupied by their fort, and the former accepted bounds not nearer than ten miles east of the Hudson river [1650]. The Duke of York's charter of 1664 conveyed to him the country between the Connecticut and Delaware rivers; and after the Dutch had been conquered, York's governor attempted to establish a claim to the country as far as the Connecticut. This, however, he was unable to do. The commissioners of 1664 determined on a boundary-line running north-northwest from tide-water in the 'Mamarouck.' But learning later that such a line would cross the Hudson in the Highlands, instead of keeping twenty miles east of that river, the same commissioners abrogated their former decision, and the dispute between the inhabitants of New York and Connecticut was renewed. In 1683 there was an agreement entered into between the parties, by which New York agreed to cede to Connecticut a tract of 61,440 acres, in return for a similar tract between the portion so set off and Massachusetts. Royal sanction to the agreement was received, and New York surveyed and set off to Connecticut the portion agreed upon; but the latter failed to do her part. In 1725 commissioners were appointed, who entered into articles of agreement as to the manner of conducting the survey, and there halted for six years. Finally in 1731, the survey was made of the portion north of that which had been set off by New York in 1684; and the line of demarcation between New York and Connecticut was fixed practically as now. Nevertheless, controversies arose from time to time regarding the boundary; and in 1860 New York made an ex parte survey, which survey was adopted by agreement between the two states in 1880, and confirmed by the Congress of the United States, on February 26, 1881.

Massachusetts compromised her claim to land in New York by allowing the present boundary-line to be established in consideration of receiving one-half of the proceeds of the sale of the public lands of that state.

The territory now forming the state of Vermont was the subject of a long and bitter struggle. Though explored and claimed by the French, they had to yield that with their other possessions in the year 1763. In the meantime a lively contest between New York and New Hampshire had developed in reference to the same district. The former insisted on having her charter limits; while under New Hampshire's seal, Wentworth, the royal governor, was granting lands between the Connecticut and Lake Champlain. Massachusetts tried also to extend her borders in this direction; but resigned her claims in 1781. In the following year New Hampshire did likewise. The inhabitants would have submitted to New York's jurisdiction if that state had recognized the validity of the New Hampshire land grants. Failing to do this, the sturdy inhabitants of the district held out for an independent state government; and succeeded finally in 1790 in wringing from New York her consent thereto.

The New Netherlands had extended their sway to the west of the Delaware in 1655. But that portion of her dominions did not prosper, and the victors did not long have the pleasure of ruling over their conquered neighbors. After nine years, the whole region falls a prey to a new conqueror, England. The agents of the Duke of York seized the settlements on the west of the Delaware as well as those on the east, although that river formed his charter bounds; and till 1681 they ruled the same as an appendage of New York. In that year a new colony is marked out which is to extend five degrees west of the Delaware River, with northern extension to " the three and fortieth degree of Northerne Latitude; and bounded on the South by a Circle drawne at twelve miles distance from New Castle Northward and Westward unto the beginning of the fortieth degree of Northern Latitude, and then by a streight Line Westward to the Limitt of Longitude above-mentioned." Read as a whole, the charter is evidently intended to grant three degrees of latitude; but taking advantage of the expression, " the said Lands to bee bounded on the North by the beginning of the three and fortieth degree of Northern Latitude," it was decided in the middle of the following century that the king could grant lands to the north of the " beginning " of the forty-third degree of latitude, which was interpreted as meaning all north of the forty-second parallel. This practically excluded Pennsylvania from the commerce of Lake Erie. But in 1781 New York released to the general government all land to which she had claim, west of the meridian of the western extremity of Lake Ontario; and the small triangle thus formed on Lake Erie was bought by the state of Pennsylvania from the general government in 1792. In the Virginia charter of 1609 occurred, in the description of the territory granted, the following expression: " and all that Space and Circuit of Land, lying from the Sea Coast of the Precinct aforesaid, up into the Land throughout from Sea to Sea, West and Northwest." Under this patent, or rather description (for the patent was at an early day abrogated), Virginia claimed for a long time the territory now comprised within the western limits of Pennsylvania: but was finally led to acquiesce in the terms of the latter's patent by which the line five degrees west of the Delaware became the western border.

Pennsylvania's southern boundary-line was the cause of a bitter quarrel with Maryland, of ninety years' duration. The charter of the latter defined her northern boundary as extending from the Delaware Bay in a direct line to the meridian of the head waters of the Potomac ; but it also provided that that line should be on the fortieth parallel of latitude. As the bay does not extend so far north as forty degrees, it was impossible to reconcile the two descriptions. Penn's territory was to be bounded on the south by a curved line, drawn at a radius of twelve miles from New Castle, and continued by the fortieth parallel ; and these two descriptions were also irreconcilable with each other. Baltimore claimed to the fortieth parallel wherever the astronomers might find it, in as much as that would give him the most territory ; while Penn, for the same reason, claimed to the twelve-mile line from New Castle. According to the rules of law the concrete, such as the mention of the Delaware Bay and the line at a fixed distance from New Castle, takes precedence of the general or imaginary, as the fortieth parallel, whose determination depends on the accuracy of the astronomical instruments used, and the skill of the observer; so that technically Penn had the better case; and the courts and Privy Council of England so decided a number of times; but the Baltimores continued to contest the matter so long as there was a possibility of gaining thereby; and the matter was not finally settled until 1767, by the survey of the famous Mason and Dixon line, which line was the result of a compromise, agreed upon by the parties to the dispute in 1732, and enforced by the English court in 1760.[1]

Nature herself had settled, on three sides, the bounds of New Jersey. But with the fourth, that colony had difficulties enough. Several months before he himself was in possession, the Duke of York granted to Carteret and Berkeley this peninsula, to be bounded " on the north by a line drawn from the Hudson at the forty-first parallel of latitude, to strike the Delaware in 41° 40'." The Peninsula was for a time divided into east and west provinces, which however in the end became united. There were numerous attempts to incorporate the whole in New York, but they ultimately failed; as did also the persistent efforts of New York to move the dividing line further toward the south; so that in consequence the first designated bounds became the permanent ones for New Jersey.

The history of the boundary-lines of Delaware is intimately connected with that of Pennsylvania, as both territories were under the rule of the same English grantee. At the same time as the southern limit of Pennsylvania was settled, Delaware's bounds were also fixed. The twelve-mile circle from the centre of New Castle was her northern boundary; her

---

[1] For details see the author's article: "The boundary dispute between Pennsylvania and Maryland." *Pennsylvania Mag. of Hist. and Biog.*, October, 1885.

8

territory was to extend so far south as the claimed position
of Cape Henlopen of the old maps, which accounts for
the discrepancy of the description with the modern maps.
From this point, a due east and west line was to be run
across the land to Chesapeake Bay, and from its centre,
a straight line was to be run tangent to the circle about
New Castle; and from the point of contact, a due north
and south line was to be carried to the southern border line
of Pennsylvania.

South of the fortieth parallel lies an immense district, the
whole of which was at first called by the English, Virginia.
Only a comparatively small portion surrounding the spot
on which was established the first permanent settlement
there, retains the name to-day. To the north lies Maryland, the first tract that became independent; of whose
north and east boundaries we have already spoken. To the
west there could be no ground of dispute, except as to that
small portion of the line between the head waters of the
Potomac and the southern line of Pennsylvania. This was
surveyed by commissioners appointed by Maryland and Virginia in 1859, and ratified by the Maryland legislature in the
year 1860; and since the formation of West Virginia, is the
border between that state and Maryland. But as to which
branch of the Potomac should be considered its head waters
continues to this day, I believe, a subject of dispute between
Maryland and Virginia. The short southern boundary-line
on the eastern peninsula was also the cause of considerable
trouble between Maryland and Virginia. In order to fill the
disputed territory with persons attached to his interest, Lord
Baltimore offered the lands here to the inhabitants of the
neighboring counties of Virginia on specially favorable terms,
which offers " appear to have been gladly accepted." In the
end however Virginia seems to have been the winner; for as
late as 1874 we find among an enumeration of Maryland's
losses, taking the bounds of the original charter as the stand-

ard,—" and to Virginia a half million of acres."[1] The final settlement was made by the award of arbitrators in 1877, which was ratified by the respective states, and at last by Congress in 1879.

As early as 1630 a large tract south of the present Virginia was granted to Sir Robert Heath ; but as no permanent settlement came into existence under his authority, the grant was afterwards declared void ; and in 1663 the Earl of Clarendon, the Duke of Albemarle, and others received a patent from the English monarch for all that tract extending from " Lucke Island, which lieth in the southern Virginia seas, and within six and thirty degrees of the northern latitude," as far south " as the river St. Matthias, which bordereth upon the coast of Florida," and west to the Pacific. In the later charter of 1665 these limits were somewhat changed, the northern extremity being placed at the north end of " Currituck river or inlet," while the southern line was extended to the twenty-ninth parallel. The influx of immigrants was for a time considerable ; and they mostly gathered round two centres, in the northern and southern portions respectively. Inspired with ideas of freedom and popular rights, they broke away not only from the proprietors, but also from each other. The border-line remained for a long time a matter of controversy ; a decision of the English authorities was reached in 1772, but failed of establishment. On attaining independence in 1776, North Carolina recognized the border line as laid down by the English authorities, and inserted it in her constitution adopted that year. It was to be a north-west line starting at the mouth of the Little River and running "through the boundary house, which stands in thirty-three degrees fifty-six seconds, to thirty-five degrees north latitude ; and from thence a west course so far as is mentioned in the Charter of King "

---

[1] Report and journal of proceedings of the joint commissioners to adjust the boundary line of the States of Maryland and Virginia. Annapolis, 1874, p. 122.

"Charles II. to the late proprietors of Carolina." South
Carolina was unwilling to accept this simple boundary-line;
and the result of disputes and defective surveying is the present
irregular one, by which North Carolina has lost "probably
between 500 and 1,000 square miles."[1] In 1789 the state
ceded to the federal government all lands to which she had
claim west of the Smoky Mountains; but the commissioners
who surveyed the southern part of the line in 1821 made it a
direct north and south line instead of following the mountains,
by which North Carolina lost a valuable mining district.

In 1732 there was carved out of South Carolina all the
country between the most northern branch of the Savannah
and the most southern branch of the Altamaha (most probably
the St. Matthias of the charter of 1663), and extending west
from their respective sources to the Pacific. To this tract was
given the name of Georgia. Trouble arising with the Spanish
colony of Florida, there was conquered and retained the post
at the mouth of the St. Mary's River. Florida itself being
ceded to England in 1763, the district between St. Mary's
and the Altamaha was formally annexed to Georgia by proclamation and has ever since continued to be a part of the same.
There were however long disputes as to which stream consti-
tutes the head of St. Mary's; and the matter was not finally
decided until the present century.

Thus we have attempted to sketch the manner in which
our national and early state boundaries became what they are.
Almost every line has a history of its own, which it would be
interesting to follow out in detail; but that would take us
much beyond the limits of a lecture.

The charters of some of the original colonies extended their
jurisdiction west to the Pacific; but this they were destined
never to enjoy. The valley of the Mississippi received French
and Spanish immigrants before English settlers made their
way thither. When France was compelled to resign Canada

---

[1] Quoted in Henry Gannett's *Boundaries of the United States*, p. 95.

in 1763, England, on the other hand, yielded all claim to territory west of the Mississippi. The United States having won their independence from the latter country, fell heir to her claims as far west as that river. There being great practical difficulties in the way of settling the conflicting claims of the several states to the immense, almost uninhabited tract, between the Appalachian Mountains and the Mississippi, Virginia led the way [1781] in offering to resign her share of the same to the national government, on condition that the territory so surrendered should in time, when sufficiently populated, be divided into states to be admitted into the Union on the same footing as the original states. This generous example was followed by other states. At first with scattered population and immense extent, there were formed territorial or temporary governments, with the main power resting in the federal government. As population increased, bounds were contracted;—natural boundary-lines where practicable being adopted ; and when no natural boundary offered itself, straight north and south, and east and west lines were generally laid down. From this point on, the subject has less interest. There was now a central power to settle the lines of demarkation ; and these were generally acquiesced in without hesitation. The territory. west of the Mississippi came by treaties, directly into the hands of the national government; and the several states as such, have had little or no voice in the matter of its division. Here was again the story of increasing population and narrowing bounds ; and where there was no international dispute, the boundary-lines of the far west present comparatively little material for the historian.

VI.

The intelligent mind has a natural curiosity to know something of the world in which we live; how much more then of the land which we call ours, to which we owe allegiance, in patriotism for which our breasts are supposed to swell with pride whenever her name is mentioned, and in defence of which we may be called upon at any moment to lay down our lives. Moreover, such a mobile population as the American, wishes to know of all parts of its country, so that each one may see if perchance he might not better his condition by going elsewhere than where he is at the time being. Then too, there is the economical consideration:—when men are hunting the treasures of the earth, a geological map may help them materially in the search. For the great nations of Europe, the chief reason for making a perfect map of their land is one of military aim, as the fate of battles is often decided by the more or less accurate knowledge of the topography of the ground whereon they are to be fought. To this end the principal nations there have had constructed maps whereon it is attempted to represent not only the main features of elevation and drainage; but it is scarcely too much to say that every farm house and every clump of trees, together with every by-path are represented. With these maps it is possible even for a stranger to go through the land without a guide, and follow his route with almost as much confidence as though he were at home there. As America changes with great rapidity in its cultural aspects, especially in the West, the United

118

States authorities have not deemed it advisable to go into such
detail here; but, though we do not expect a war, as do the
nations of Europe, and can therefore spare the expense of such
minute work, the surveying that had already been done before
the opening of the War of the Rebellion was found very
useful to the authorities during the war; and the Survey has
been more popular and has secured the support of Congress
in a much more liberal spirit ever since. Another object,
which in Europe leads to the making of accurate national
maps, but is of little importance here, is for taxing purposes.
Where the population is crowded together, and the expenses
of government great in proportion to the national wealth, it
becomes important to be able to tax everything which will
bear it; and land has been in all countries an important
source of revenue to the government; as population increases,
the value of land per square foot gains in importance, and an
accurate knowledge of the possibilities of the revenues is
necessary to the authorities. Though our national government
lays no tax on land in private hands, the same is generally
subject to local taxation; and, as the best surveys in the
country are those of the central authorities, several of the
state governments have called in the assistance of the central
power in surveying their domains. This country's immense
coast-line, in connection with its great natural wealth, destined
it for a land of large commercial interests; and in furtherance
of these interests it is necessary to do what is possible for the
safety of the shipping engaged in the carrying trade. Accordingly a knowledge of the coast of the country is of paramount
importance. This is not to be had for the mere asking;
because the gaining of that knowledge must come through
work of the most delicate and complicated kind. Not only
must the line between land and water be laid down, and that
varies from hour to hour on account of the tides; but the
points on the land by which the position of a ship nearing the
shore can be determined, must also be accurately mapped. To
this add the necessity of knowing the channels by which the

shore may be safely approached, the direction of the currents
through which one must pass, and which have an influence on
the sailing of the ship ; and still more, the depth of water at
a given time, as that is equally important ; and it will be seen
how necessary it is for a commercial country to have a
coast survey.

How are maps made ? is a very natural question, after one
has been talking so much about the product. The method
pursued depends very largely on the object aimed at. The
maps of some of the early navigators serve as an illustration
of what may be done by personal observation of a country,
with little or no assistance from instruments. With training,
one may acquire the power of observing closely and repro-
ducing fairly well what one has seen. An army officer told
me at Washington, that men are now trained in our army so
that after riding over the country they can on their return
make a very fair sketch of the topography of the land seen,
and sufficiently accurate to enable a commander to place his
troops for a battle, dispose his artillery to advantage, etc.
But on such reconnaisances, as they are called, no accurate
maps could be based. A step higher in the scale of accuracy
are the ordinary plane surveys, such as are used in platting
land for the market, or city building lots. Though this
method is sufficiently accurate for short distances, it is utterly
inadequate for long distances, owing to the spheroidal form
of the earth ; as, for example, a survey continued in this
manner from the Gulf of Mexico to the northern boundary of
the State of Mississippi, would there be in error four miles in
every hundred.

Up to a comparatively recent period, the best maps of the
United States were almost entirely based on such surveys, as
no other kind had been carried out to any extent. Separate
portions of the country had been thus surveyed, as was thought,
with sufficient accuracy ; but when it was attempted to unite
into one whole the several maps thus produced, they were
found not to fit, and some strange results were noted ; as for

example the Ohio River disappeared, while the Mississippi
was almost annihilated in some places, and in others its width
increased to several miles. For really accurate surveying, it
is necessary to have a geodetic foundation, that is, all lines
must be considered in reference to the curvature of the earth's
surface. Work of this kind requires a knowledge of higher
mathematics, together with skill in using instruments of
the utmost delicacy for astronomical and terrestrial observation. The foundation of this work is in the astronomical determination of the position of two or more points on the surface
of the earth ; for the earth being spherical, there is no other
method of determining absolute position on it than in reference
to the heavens ; and even this is not infallible, as the improvement in methods and instruments of one age has shown the
errors of the preceding. But it is the best we have, and must
therefore be the basis of the best work. The amount of labor
involved in such determination of position may be judged from
the fact that Mechain and Delambre, two famous French
surveyors, each made 1800 astronomical observations to ascer-
tain the exact position of the Pantheon at Paris. Then there
must be a base-line measured on the earth, for which work
many instruments have been invented, with ever increasing
accuracy ; so that now it is maintained that the experts can
measure a mile on the ground with a probable error of only
one-quarter of an inch or less. This line must be connected by
triangles with the points astronomically determined ; and each
angle of every triangle is, on the average, measured thirty
times by those engaged on the U. S. Coast Survey. But even
this is not all, for the altitude of every point must be known
and then reduced to the level of the sea. In determining the
size and form of the earth, to which all this work naturally
leads, it is not the form as presented to the eye, but an
imaginary form, such as there would be if the entire globe
were covered with a calm ocean. Only with such a beginning
is it possible to prepare a correct map of the country. The
further work to be done depends on the object for which the

survey is made.   If that is for a general map of a country, such as you find in the ordinary atlas, only a comparatively few points need to be thus established, and the rest can be drawn in after less careful observations of the intervening country.   If the utmost accuracy is sought, then it becomes necessary to observe with great care an almost innumerable number of triangles, and to pass over practically every foot of the ground, and note its configuration.   The work of our national government furnishes us with illustrations of all the varieties of surveying now in use ; for, with various objects in view at different times, the government has instituted surveys of all grades of accuracy.   For ordinary geographical purposes the survey should be of such a character as to give, when complete, a knowledge of the distribution of land and water, of the elevations of the land, of the position of political borders, and the situation of cities and towns.   Going beyond this, it is possible to have maps of an infinite variety, showing the distribution of the population, or of the mineral resources, or of rainfall,—in short, of an endless variety of matters of information.

    In the prosecution of this work there are needed not only men of trained minds capable of doing the work, but also elaborate instruments for the necessary observations ; first for the determination of the latitude, which is now done principally by observing stars near the zenith, instead of circumpolar stars, as was originally the case; in which work, the Americans have made some advances on that of their predecessors.   Then the longitude is to be determined, in which our experts have shown the world how it can be done with the greatest accuracy, namely, by means of the electric telegraph. In perhaps no branch of science has the advance been greater since the discovery of America, than just here ; for the early navigators were liable to mistakes of from fifteen to twenty degrees in its determination ; while, for example, the Coast Survey has determined the longitude of Lafayette Park, San Francisco, by several sets of experiments whose results differ from each other but 0.06 of a second of time or 0.90 of a second of arc ; or less than $\frac{1}{3800}$ of the error of the early navigators. Of very great importance is also the manner, as well as the means, of measuring the base-lines ; because an inaccuracy here will extend throughout the whole line dependent on it, in the same proportion. For this work new instruments have been invented and constructed at Washington, in the manipulation of which there has been distinguished success. In the observation of the angles of the triangles by which the survey is conducted, Americans have reached as high a degree of accuracy as any other nation ; and have observed the greatest distance ever used for such purpose, in one case, the two stations being one hundred and ninety-one miles apart. After all the innumerable observations have been made, there follows the intricate work of bringing the results thus obtained into shape for the construction of the map, which is the ultimate object aimed at. Now the artists are brought into requisition, who are to place on paper, correctly and in a manner agreeable to the eye and also easy of comprehension, all that has been learned by the survey. This done, the picture must be transferred to stone or copper and placed in the hands of the printer. From him it passes to the public, who as a rule have not the slightest conception of the vast amount of labor that has been expended on its production.

It will probably be easier to understand what the government has done, after having an idea of the problems which it was desired to solve ; hence this, perhaps too long, introduction. The attention of the federal government was called to the need of a survey of the coast as early as 1806, by Professor Patterson, of Philadelphia, who, it is believed, was the originator of the idea. President Jefferson recognized the value of the suggestion and sent to Congress a recommendation in accordance therewith. This resulted in the law of 1807 by which the President was authorized to inaugurate a survey of the coast. The plan of work submitted by Mr. Hassler, a Swiss who had been engaged in similar work in his

native land, was accepted; and he was authorized to go to
Europe in order to procure the necessary instruments. There
were unavoidable delays in making the preliminary preparations, and it was 1811 before Mr. Hassler departed on his
mission. Then came the war with great Britain, and other
complications arose, so that he did not return with the necessary equipment until 1816, and the work of surveying was
commenced the year following. But Congress felt dissatisfied
with the slow progress of its measure, and refused, after two
years, to renew its appropriation, so that the work was compelled to cease in 1819. From this time until 1832, what
little was done toward increasing the knowledge of our coast-
line was done by the navy, but so poorly that Congress was
finally induced to revive the old law, and Mr. Hassler was
again placed in charge. The work was now reorganized in a
more efficient manner, and continued under the same direction
until Mr. Hassler's death in 1843. But it was not free from
fault-finding criticism during this time, and had to undergo
a searching investigation in 1842, from which it emerged in
triumph. When it is considered that Mr. Hassler had to
organize the work from the foundation, train his assistants,
and in some cases even invent his own instruments, it will be
found that the work he accomplished in the ten years preceding the investigation was most creditable to him. The results
are thus summarized by one of his successors : " A base-line
had been measured in the vicinity of New York, the commercial importance of which obviously indicated it as the
proper point of beginning. The triangulation had extended
eastward to Rhode Island and southward to the head of Chesapeake Bay, the primary triangulation crossing the neck of
New Jersey and Delaware, while a secondary triangulation
skirted the coast of New Jersey, meeting with another series
which extended down Delaware Bay. The topography had
kept pace with the triangulation, and the hydrography of New
York bay and harbor, of Long Island Sound, of Delaware
bay and river, and the off-shore soundings from Montauk "

" Point to the capes of the Delaware were substantially completed. The triangulation covered an area ' of 9000 square
miles, furnishing determinations of nearly 1200 stations for
the delineation of 1600 miles of shore-line; 168 topographical
maps had been surveyed and 142 hydrographical charts.' "
[Johnson's Cyclopaedia, Art. Coast Survey.]

The act of March 10th, 1843, provided that the Coast
Survey be organized on a plan to be submitted by a commission appointed by the President of the United States, and
to consist of three civilians, two officers of the navy, and four
of the army. These had already completed their task by the
end of the same month; and on the 30th, submitted to the
President, " The Plan for the reorganization of the Coast
Survey." Professor A. D. Bache was the new director; and
throughout the period of almost a quarter of a century, during
which he occupied that important position, the Survey continued the work with great proficiency. During this period the
United States doubled its coast-line by the acquisition of
Mexican territory, and the settlement of the Oregon dispute;
so that there was all the more necessity for increasing the
facilities of the bureau. In 1867 Mr. Bache died, and was
succeeded by Professor Benjamin Pierce; and in the same
year, Alaska was purchased from Russia, by which 26,000
miles more were added to the national coast-line. It is the
duty of the Coast Survey to delineate accurately the entire
line of the national coast, with all its meanderings, including
all bays, and rivers up to the head of tide-water, as well as the
adjacent islands. Taking this view of it, our Atlantic coast
has a length of 14,723 miles; that of the Gulf of Mexico,
10,406 miles; and the Pacific coast, exclusive of Alaska, 4,252
miles; so that, including Alaska, the work of this bureau
must cover an extent of more than 55,000 miles. Nor is this
all; for their work extends inland as far as may be useful for
coast defense; and out to sea, twenty leagues, and sometimes
further; as in investigating the Gulf Stream. Furthermore
they have extended a geodetic line along the Appalachian

Mountains; and lines of level even to the mouth of the Mississippi, by which it is shown that the Gulf of Mexico is 40 inches higher at the latter point, than the ocean at Cape Cod, —a most important discovery which suggests at once a theory as to the cause of the movement of the Gulf Stream. And lastly, they are running a geodetic line from the Atlantic to the Pacific, as a trustworthy basis for the accurate geography of the interior. Of this enormous stretch of country there now (March 1st, 1892) remain to be surveyed only eight degrees of longitude,—some portions of Kansas and Colorado, and one station in Utah, being still unfinished.

Notwithstanding the high quality of the work done by this bureau, which has received the approval and praise of scientists in Europe and America, there have not been wanting from time to time detractors, who have made charges of inefficiency, generally coupled with the demand that the oversight of the bureau be transferred to another department of the government, namely the Navy—it has generally been a sub-division of the Treasury Department. But from each new investigation, it has come out with increased honor; and instead of doing it harm, the attention aroused by such carping has only added to its good name.

By the kindness of Professor T. C. Mendenhall, the present Director of the Survey, I have been placed in possession of a manuscript copy of an article entitled: " The U. S. Coast and Geodetic Survey. Summary of its History, Objects, Methods of Work and Contributions to Geographical Knowledge," from which I extract the following, as to some of the results of this gigantic undertaking of our government: " In the introduction of improved instruments, apparatus and methods of observation, marked progress was made. The primary base-lines were measured with an apparatus devised by the Superintendent and constructed at the Office of the Survey with special reference to accuracy and economy of measurement and facility of use in the field. The method of determining latitude by measuring with a micrometer small "

" zenith differences of stars north and south of the zenith, as devised by Capt. Talcott, of the U. S. Engineers by an ingenious adaptation of the Zenith Telescope, was brought into general use in the Survey, and it was soon found by discussion of the results that the places of stars thus obtained were in many cases superior in precision to those of the British Association Catalogue. This led to a demand for better star places, and at the request of the Superintendent, the Directors of the principal Observatories undertook to determine the places of all stars observed by the Coast Survey for latitude. Not only was the accuracy of the latitude determinations of the Survey thus increased, but the Observatories themselves felt the stimulus given to astronomical research, and to the publication of Star Catalogues of a high order of precision."

" But the most important contribution made by the Coast Survey to practical astronomy was undoubtedly the application of the electric telegraph to the determination of differences of longitude. It was part of the plan of re-organization of 1843 that the difference of longitude between some main points of the Survey, and the meridians of any or all of the European observatories should be ascertained immediately. The Observatory at Cambridge, Massachusetts, having been adopted as the point of reference for Coast Survey longitudes, arrangements were at once carried into effect for the transportation of chronometers between Liverpool and Boston ; occultations and moon culminations were observed regularly at Cambridge, Nantucket, and Philadelphia ; and care was taken to have observations made whenever they occurred."

" As soon as the first lines of electric telegraph were established, experiments were made at the suggestion of Professor Bache, and with the co-operation of Professor Morse, between Washington and Philadelphia and Philadelphia and New York. The Coast Survey Report for 1846 contains an account of the first successful attempt made to exchange signals for longitude, by the electric telegraph. On the 10th of October in that year communication was effected between "

" Philadelphia and Washington ; signals for time by the clock were transmitted, and the instant of transit of a star over the wires of the transit instrument was telegraphed. From this date each year brought improvements in methods of observing and recording ; the signals were soon recorded automatically by astronomical clocks upon chronographs. The Atlantic Cable of 1866 was at once utilized as a means of determining the longitude of Cambridge from Greenwich ; in 1870, a second determination was made through the French Cables from Brest to Duxbury, Mass., the cables being joined at St. Pierre, Miquelon ; and in 1872, Brest having been connected with Greenwich by cable, signals from Cambridge, from Greenwich and from Paris were united at Brest and compared on the Brest chronograph, and a satisfactory junction effected between the American and European systems of longitude."

" From the final discussion of the results of these three determinations, made in different years and by different observers, it appears that the several values for the longitude of Cambridge from Greenwich do not differ more than five-hundredths of a second of time.

" The distinguished astronomer Sir George B. Airy, Director of the Greenwich Observatory, was among the first to recognize the great value of the American method, as it soon came to be called, and to adopt it in the work under his charge. It is now in general use by astronomers throughout the world. In North America, the stations connected by telegraphic determinations of longitude extend from Newfoundland to Mexico and Central America, and from the Atlantic to the Pacific. Upwards of one hundred and forty such stations have been occupied in the United States."

The survey of the Atlantic and Gulf coast-lines is practically complete. As to what still remains to be done on the Pacific, I cannot do better than quote Professor Mendenhall himself. In a letter of March 1st, 1892, he says: " The portions of the Pacific Coast remaining to be surveyed are as follows:—The primary triangulation from about latitude 40° "

"to the vicinity of Olympia, Washington; the coast triangulation from the vicinity of Cape Sebastian to and including the Straits of Fuca, excepting detached portions in the vicinity of Coos Bay, Willapa Bay, Gray's Harbor, Umbqua and Yaquina rivers, etc.; the topography of the outer coasts of Oregon and Washington is about one-third completed, but a preliminary or reconnaissance survey has been made over the whole. The various harbors and entrances are completed. The Straits of Fuca and some portions of the Gulf of Georgia are still unfinished. The hydrography from Cape Orford to Cape Kiwanda, Oregon, and from Gray's Harbor to Cape Johnson, Washington, remain to be surveyed. In south-east Alaska all the waters between the main-land and the islands, and including Portland Canal, from Dixon Entrance to the head of Chilcat Inlet have been surveyed, but all other portions of the Alaska coast remain unsurveyed."

I cannot say just what amount of money this great work has cost; but in a pamphlet of 1884, entitled, " The late attacks upon the Coast and Geodetic Survey," p. 16, there is the following statement: " The average appropriation . . . from 1870 to 1884,—including fourteen fiscal years,—has been $622,200." " For the current fiscal year (1891–92), the appropriation for field and office expenses, repairs of vessels, Alaska Boundary Survey, &c., is $515,130." Besides the paid officials of the Coast Survey, army and navy officers have from time to time been detailed by their respective superiors to assist in the work; but at present none of the army are so engaged, though some navy officers are detailed by the Navy Department for hydrographic work conducted by the Coast Survey.

When we are told that 53,000 copies of charts were issued by this bureau last year (1891), it enables us to form some slight conception of the large scale on which its work is carried on. These charts are of different varieties, both as to methods of presenting the facts with which they deal, and also as to the amount of detail given thereon. In scale they range between 1 : 5000 and 1 : 80,000. The average of the maps,

9

however, are made on a scale of 1 : 10,000, or about 6 inches to the mile; so that a square foot on the map represents about four square miles of the earth's surface. As the maps are made for navigators, but little of the land is shown, but that little is given with great minuteness; and hill and valley, woods and fields, roads, railroads, and water ways down to the smallest creek,—all find place here. Then too every light house with the color of its light, every buoy with its color, the route for the safest approach to land, with its compass direction and the variation of the compass, soundings at innumerable points, together with the substance and character of the bottom,—all can here be seen at a glance and be much better and more easily understood than from a lengthy description in words. A map of the entire United States on such a scale ($\frac{1}{10000}$) would require four hundred thousand sheets, which in atlas form, would constitute a library of itself, of eight thousand large folio volumes.

Though scientifically unimportant, the plane survey of the public lands of the United States has been of great commercial utility. In 1802 Colonel Mansfield, then surveyor of the Northwest Territory, proposed a plan for the carrying out of this work, which plan with small variations, has been in use ever since. The public domain is divided into land districts, over each of which there is placed a surveyor-general, whose duty it is to superintend the survey thereof. In each district a meridian and an east and west line are carefully run, and their positions determined astronomically, though not with the utmost accuracy. With this as a foundation, the whole district is divided into townships, six miles square, a conventional allowance being made for the true direction of the meridians. Smaller divisions, called sections, quarter-sections, etc., are surveyed as the land is put on the market. Large portions of the country have been thus surveyed, with varying degrees of accuracy. "Unfortunately, one vicious principle was early incorporated in the plan, viz., that the work should be given out under contract, not to the lowest bidder but to" "preferred bidders, a method which resulted in great extravagance on the one hand, and such a deterioration of the work upon the other that it finally subserved but the single purpose of parceling the lands. Since the organization of these surveys up to the present time (1884) $35,000,000 have been expended therefor, and it will always be a matter of profound regret to scholars and statesmen that the grand purposes for which the surveys were primarily organized were not fully realized." (J. W. Powell, On the Organization of Scientific Work of the General Government, Pt. 2, p. 1072.)

Previous to the organization of the Geological Survey in 1879, the work of surveying the country was distributed among various bodies of experts. Thus to the Lake Survey, was entrusted the work of surveying the shores of the Great Lakes and connecting Lake Michigan with the head of Lake Erie. To the Engineers' Corps of the army was given the work of surveying several small areas of land, the course of the Mississippi, and other places for the improvement of rivers. The early explorations of the west were made by parties sent out by the War Department. These parties made maps of the country seen, but they were necessarily crude; and they are now of but little use. Some of the older States undertook to have their own domains surveyed, among which were New Hampshire, Massachusetts, New York, New Jersey, Pennsylvania, and North Carolina. Then too the surveys necessary for the great railroads increased very considerably the accurate knowledge of the topography of the country, some of this work having been done with great care.

After the War of the Rebellion, the national government entered on this class of work with more vigor than it had hitherto displayed, and the work was prosecuted in several localities at the same time. Under Mr. Clarence King, the fortieth parallel between the one hundred and fourth and the one hundred and twentieth meridian west from Greenwich was surveyed, including a strip of land one hundred and five miles wide, and covering in all an area of 87,000 square miles.

Of this region a map was made, representing four miles to the inch, with contour lines representing vertical differences of three hundred feet.

About 100,000 square miles of country in Colorado, New Mexico, Wyoming, Utah, and Idaho were surveyed by the Geological and Geographical Survey of the Territories, under the direction of Dr. F. V. Hayden. Maps of this survey were also issued, of the same scale as that of King, but with the contour lines at every 200 feet.

"The Geographical Surveys west of the One Hundredth Meridian" were placed under the charge of Lieut. George M. Wheeler of the Engineer Corps; and several hundred thousand square miles in Colorado, New Mexico, Arizona, Nevada, California, Oregon, and Idaho were surveyed; but on so small a scale and by such inaccurate methods that the work does not at all meet the modern requirements, and much of it will have to be done over again.

In Wyoming, Utah, and Arizona, about 60,000 square miles were surveyed by a body of men under the able direction of the present head of the Geological Survey, of which a map was made on a scale of four miles to the inch, and 250 feet contours. The aggregate cost of these four surveys was only $1,985,028.57,—less than is now expended in two years for the operations of the Coast and Geodetic Survey and the Geological Survey.

Experience however showed that such division of labor was not advantageous, either from an economical point of view, or as regards the quality of the work. Accordingly in 1879, after mature consideration, all these various surveys were abolished, and the entire work of this nature, excepting that of the Coast and Geodetic Survey, which serves a different purpose, and proceeds largely on different methods, was united under the management of the Geological Survey; so that since then all such work has been carried on in accordance with a unified plan, and under the same central control.

" For convenience of administration, but controlled by geologic considerations, the area of the United States is divided into seven districts, as follows : "

I. District of the North Atlantic, comprising Maine, New Hampshire, Vermont, Massachusetts, Rhode Island, Connecticut, New York, New Jersey, Pennsylvania, Delaware, Maryland, and the District of Columbia.

II. District of the South Atlantic, comprising Virginia, North Carolina, South Carolina, Georgia, Florida, Alabama, Tennessee, Kentucky, and West Virginia.

III. District of the North Mississippi, comprising Ohio, Indiana, Illinois, Michigan, Wisconsin, Minnesota, Dakota, Nebraska, Kansas, Iowa, and Missouri.

IV. District of the South Mississippi, comprising Indian Territory, Arkansas, Mississippi, Louisiana, and Texas.

V. District of the Rocky Mountains, comprising Montana, Wyoming, Colorado, part of Utah, New Mexico, and part of Arizona.

VI. District of the Great Basin, comprising parts of Washington Territory, Oregon, California, Utah, Arizona, Nevada, and Idaho.

VII. District of the Pacific, comprising part of Washington Territory, part of Oregon, and the greater portion of California.[1]

The entire work of the survey is divided into four main classes, topographic, geologic, paleontologic, and chemic,—to use the expressions of the official reports. Though the whole is subordinated to the geological work, from which the organization takes its name, the topographical work must precede the rest as a foundation on which all that follows is built; for it is evident that you must have an idea of the lay of the land before you can represent the geological formations of the country in their true relations. With the great extent of the country, it is manifest that it is not possible to be surveying

---

[1] Fourth Annual Report of the U. S. Geolog. Survey, Introduction.

in all parts of it at the same time, and the work was accordingly commenced in those regions where valuable deposits of minerals enforced the demand for a knowledge of the same. Originally the survey was intended only for the public domain of the general government; but since 1871 Congress has authorized work to be done in the older states as well; and in the case of Massachusetts and other states which were interested in having an exceptionally good survey of their territory, the work has been done under the direction of the Geological Survey, the interested state, however, paying the extra cost thereby incurred. On the topographical maps which are made from these surveys, are represented the natural characteristics of the country, "its mountains, hills, valleys, streams, bodies of water, etc.,—together with certain cultural features, such as highways, boundary lines of townships, counties, states, etc."[1]

When this work is done the maps are given into the hands of the geologists, for their additions. Major Powell informs us that "In later years topographic methods and plans of mapping have been changed, and these changes are radical, and are due to the influence of geologists, who have demanded better maps than those of the old military engineers."[2] With these improved maps the geologists wander hither and thither over the ground, correcting the topography where necessary, and noting the geological formations to a very minute degree, establishing "millions of points" where the geodetic survey establishes but hundreds.

There are also subdivisions of the work of geology, which are of sufficient importance to be ranked practically as separate sciences; this is especially true of paleontology, the "science which treats of the structure, affinities, classification, and distribution in time of the forms of plant and animal life embedded in the rocks of the earth's crust."[3] And for this

---

[1] Testimony before the Joint Commission, p. 184.
[2] *Ibid.*, 168.   [3] *Encyc. Brit.*, X, 319.

work there is a division of the Geological Survey; as there is also for the study of the chemical properties of the rocks and minerals which form our portion of the earth's surface.

In the work of triangulation which forms the basis of the topographical survey of this as of the Coast and Geodetic Survey, the margin of error here allowed is greater, and accordingly, the extreme delicacy of work that is so characteristic of the former is not here required. The difference in the degree of accuracy reached by the two organizations is thus summarized by Major Powell : " Just what degree of refinement is actually attained by the two organizations can be set forth better by a few illustrations. In the Coast Survey work the probable error in the length of the Kent Island base, in Chesapeake Bay, is $\frac{1}{335000}$th part of its length ; of the Peach Tree base, near Atlanta, $\frac{1}{561850}$th part of its length. In the Geological Survey the probable error of the Wingate base is $\frac{1}{150000}$th part of its length ; of the Malvern base in Arkansas, $\frac{1}{170000}$th part of its length. Errors in triangulation are defined in terms of arc, and relate to the closure of triangles. The errors in the triangulation of the Coast Survey from the Peach Tree base are not more than half a second for each angle. In the Geological Survey the average error in the closure of triangles, in all of that work in the Appalachian Mountains, executed in 1882, 1883, and 1884, is less than 8 seconds for each angle. The probable average error of lengths of lines measured by the Coast Survey from the Kent Island base is stated to be about one-half an inch in a mile. The probable average error in the lines measured by the Geological Survey in the triangulation in the Southern Appalachians is about 6 inches to the mile, *i. e.*, in a line 20 miles in length the error would probably be 10 feet." [1]

Exclusive of Alaska, the United States cover an area of about 3,000,000 square miles, of which territory more than 900,000 square miles have already been surveyed. Of this

---

[1] J. W. Powell, *Testimony*, etc., 205–6.

area there were surveyed before the present organization 384,890 square miles, to which the U. S. Geological Survey added by the end of June, 1891, 392,584 square miles ; and a letter of Nov. 3d, 1889, from Mr. Henry Gannett says : " The area surveyed by the Geological Survey up to the present date is approximately 537,000 square miles." This work produces vast results outside of the field of geography, and hence outside the range of our discussion ; but we cannot refrain from calling attention to the scientific value of the products of this branch of our governmental activity. For instance, mineral deposits of great extent and untold worth have been thereby brought to light; in the chemical department, the difference between iron and steel, which so long eluded the keen eye of the investigator, was discovered ; and even the occult processes, by which Nature forms her mineral deposits, have been largely revealed.

One of the most important fields of activity of this bureau is that of publishing the results of its extensive and multifarious labors. According to the statute approved March 3, 1879, " The publications of the Geological Survey shall consist of the annual report of operations, geological and economic maps illustrating the resources and classification of the lands, and reports upon general and economic geology and and paleontology." [1] Of these publications, those which interest us especially are the maps ; and in this direction, our government stands second to none in the beauty and practicability of its cartographical productions. Many experiments have been tried as to the best methods of engraving and printing these maps, which have resulted in the adoption of a system at once artistic, practical and economical. The topographical maps are constructed on " varying scales, but chiefly the three following, viz. : one two hundred and fifty thousandth, or about four miles to the inch ; one one hundred and twenty-five thousandth, or about two miles to the inch ;"

---

[1] Powell, *Testimony*, etc., 674.

"one sixty-two thousand five hundredth, or about one mile to the inch;"[1] and some are constructed on larger scales, when the nature of the territory requires it.   Most of the territory will be represented on the scale first mentioned, on sheets 20 by 16½ inches, so that each sheet will represent one degree of latitude and longitude.   In December, 1884, Major Powell calculated that it would take about twenty-four years to finish the work, and the map of the entire country, when complete, would require about 2,600 sheets.   A member of the surveying corps told me that since that statement of the head of the Survey, the plan of work had been somewhat changed, and the methods refined, so that although the appropriations of the last few years have been enormous, thus greatly facilitating the work, and rendering greater speed possible, that the work will doubtless require still twenty years to come for its completion.

The uses of these topographical maps are various; but one chief use will scarcely occur to those living on the Atlantic seaboard, namely, the solution of the great problem of irrigating our almost limitless western plains.   We are told that almost two-fifths of the soil of the United States requires irrigation before it will produce crops; and furthermore, that these maps convey the information on which can be based the necessary plans for the construction of the necessary works of irrigation.   It is somewhat surprising to hear that quite a number of towns in the west have been moved twice or oftener on account of error in selecting their sites; and that this might have been obviated by acquaintance with such information as these maps with their contour lines contain.   Of equal importance is perhaps the fact that thereby the only feasible method of obviating the destructive floods of the lower Mississippi has been discovered; at least, such is the claim of Major Powell.   He believes that the survey has revealed a method by which the waters sent down the Missouri and its

---

[1] *Ibid.,* 205.

branches from the melting snows of the Rocky Mountains, can be collected and stored up for the irrigation of a vast territory now arid, by want of water ; and that the same process would relieve the lower Mississippi of its over-abundance of water and render this great flood-plain "one of the most fertile districts in the United States, on which corn, cotton and sugar could be produced in vast quantities."

The other publications of the Geological Survey are doubtless in their several fields as important as those just mentioned ; but they do not belong to our theme. Enough has been said, it is hoped, to show that in its geographical work, our government is fully abreast of the best performances of the times; Major Powell goes even further and affirms that "the practice of European governments is steadily following the precedents established in the United States."

SUPPLEMENT.

It has been generally assumed by modern historians that the Mississippi river was the stream known among the Spaniards by the name Rio del Espiritu Santo, or some modification thereof. Some writers add that it was discovered and so named in 1519 by Alonso Alvarez Pineda, who was sent out that year on an exploring expedition by Francisco de Garay, Governor of Jamaica. Accordingly, it was a matter of great surprise to me, as the idea gradually assumed form, in examining the Kohl Collection of maps, in the State Department at Washington, that the usual interpretation was at least open to doubt. Hence the subject seemed worthy of a more careful consideration than has heretofore been given it ; and an examination of many maps and writings leads me to the conviction that in all probability the Mississippi was NOT discovered by Pineda, and that the early Spaniards did NOT know that river under the name of Espiritu Santo ; but that, on the contrary, they applied this name generally, if not exclusively, to the stream which now bears, in its different parts, the names Coosa, Alabama, and Mobile.

That the old idea still obtains currency is shown by the fact that the very latest work on American history, which treats of the matter, namely, that by Professor John Fiske, The Discovery of America, gives it place in the following passage :— " Pineda then turned back, and after a while entered the mouth of the Mississippi, which he called the Rio de Santo Espiritu. . . . How far he ascended it is not clear, but he"

139

"spent six weeks upon its waters and its banks, trading with the Indians, who seemed friendly and doubtless labored under the usual first impression as to the supernatural character of the white men." [II, 487.] Mr. Winsor, in his recent work on Columbus, is not so positive in his statement as Professor Fiske, but he does not express any doubt on the subject. He speaks in reference to Pineda's and other early expeditions to the northern shores of the Gulf of Mexico as follows :—" In 1519 Pineda had made the circuit of the northern shores of the Gulf of Mexico, and at the river Panuco he had been challenged by Cortes as trenching on his government. Turning again eastward, Pineda found the mouth of the river named by him Del Espiritu Santo, which passes with many modern students as the first indication in history of the great Mississippi, while others trace the first signs of that river to Cabeça de Vaca in 1528, or to the passage higher up its current by De Soto in 1541. Believing it at first the long-looked-for strait to pass to the Indies, Pineda entered it, only to be satisfied that it must gather the watershed of a continent, which in this part was now named Amichel." [p. 560.] In his Narrative and Critical History, however, Mr. Winsor admits that the subject is at least open to doubt; for in a note to page 292, volume II, he uses the expression, " even if we do not accept the view that Alonzo de Pineda found its mouth in 1519 and called it Rio del Espiritu Santo." But his doubt is rather as to whom the first discovery of the Mississipi is to be attributed than as to the identity of the Rio del Espiritu Santo with the Mississippi. That Mr. Winsor is not opposed to the idea of accepting them as identical is shown by the fact that he accepted and printed statements to that effect in the contribution of Mr. John Gilmary Shea to his Narrative and Critical History. In volume second of that work we find the statement of their identity made at least four times by that author, namely, twice on page 237, and once each on pages 247 and 282. One quotation will be sufficient to show that Mr. Shea did not share the editor's doubt as to the discovery of Pineda; for in reference to it he makes the assertion that he "discovered a river of very great volume, evidently the Mississippi." [p. 237.] In his earlier work on the Discovery and Exploration of the Mississippi Valley, Mr. Shea goes further, and actually substitutes the name Mississippi for Espiritu Santo where the latter is used by the Spanish writers. On page xi of the Introduction, referring to the expedition of De Soto, he says:—" The Mississippi, under the name of Espiritu Santo, was not unknown to him [*i. e.* De Soto]; for . . . he sent Maldonado back to Havana, with orders to meet him in six months at the mouth of the Mississippi." As the name Mississippi seems never to have been used by the Spaniards until after its adoption by the French, the order of De Soto could not possibly have read thus.

In the last revision of the great work of George Bancroft, I do not find that he says just in so many words that the Mississippi and the Rio del Espiritu Santo are one and the same river, but he does so by implication. For, in describing the territory known as the Quivira of Coronado, which lay between the Mississippi and the Rocky Mountains, he tells us, " It was well watered by brooks and rivers, which flowed to what the Spaniards then called the Espiritu Santo." [I. 36.]

To Mr. B. F. French, we owe the publication of many valuable documents relating to the exploration and settlement of Louisiana, who has even taken the trouble to print English translations of some of the valuable old French and Spanish papers. In one of his foot-notes there occurs this statement : " Alonzo Alvarez de Pineda was ordered by Francisco de Garay, Governor of Jamaica, in 1519, to explore the coast of the Gulf of Mexico, and in sailing along the coast he discovered the mouths of the Mississippi." [*Coll.*, 2d Ser., p. 242.]

A third of a century ago, the greatest authority on American historical geography was unquestionably Dr. J. G. Kohl, to whose industry and talent we owe the valuable collection of historical maps in the Department of State at Washington, and who in 1860 published fac-similes of the two famous

Spanish maps of 1527 and 1529 now preserved at Weimar. Accompanying the fac-similes is an elaborate dissertation on the contents and history of the maps. On several occasions he gives voice to his belief in the identity of the Mississippi and the Espiritu Santo, but on none more unequivocally than in the following passage, translated from page 79 :—"And it is also without doubt, that all following Spanish geographers and historians applied the name Rio del Espiritu Santo, introduced by Pineda, to the Rio Grande de Florida, discovered in the interior by De Soto in 1542 [*sic*], which is our Mississippi."

Although the consensus of opinion among modern historians is, as we have seen, in favor of considering the Rio del Espiritu Santo identical with the Mississippi, it is true that Mr. Winsor has in one place expressed a doubt, at least as to the identity of the Bay of Espiritu Santo, where he says, " Beaujeu steered, as he thought, for the Baye du St. Esprit (Mobile Bay [?])" [IV. 237.] Mr. Shea in his work on the Discovery of the Mississippi Valley, referring to the same expedition, that of La Salle trying to reach the Mississippi by sea, makes another guess as to the bay then sought under the name of Espiritu Santo, and thinks it the " Appalachee." [p. 190.]

Both Professor Fiske and Mr. Winsor make the statement that Pineda named the river he discovered the Rio del Espiritu Santo ; and the latter even refers to his authority for the description in which the statement occurs, namely, Navarrete, III. 64. Professor Fiske, however, does not here indulge his readers' curiosity as to his sources of information. What shall we say, then, to the fact that Navarrete, in his description of the expedition of Pineda, entirely fails to name the Rio del Espiritu Santo, or give any other name to the river at whose mouth Pineda made so long a stay. He merely describes it as "a river of very great volume," then proceeds with the history of the expedition. As there are several other points which are of value in determining whether or not

Pineda was on the Mississippi, a literal translation of the passage that contains the pith of the matter in question is here given.

The expedition, having gone east and west, and taken possession of the country in the name of the King, " they turned back and entered a river of very great volume, at the mouth of which there was a large town where they stayed more than forty days, repairing the ships and trading with the natives, in the most friendly and amicable manner. They travelled six leagues up the river and saw forty towns on the shores. This was called the province of Amichel: good land, quiet, healthy, well stored with provisions and fruits: its inhabitants wore many ornaments of gold in their noses and ears." [Navarrete, III. 65.] It will be observed that a river is here mentioned and described, but not named. The description furnishes, moreover, an argument tending to show that this river was not the Mississippi.

As to the river being " of very great volume," that is a characteristic too general to fix the river where Pineda made his long halt; for we must remember that the Spaniards of that day were not familiar with such great rivers as the Amazon and the Mississippi; and accordingly used such expressions as the above, in describing much smaller streams. For instance, Cortes called the Panuco, a "great river," the very term that was applied to the Mississippi when its true greatness was known, although we should consider the Panuco but a small stream. However, the second statement, namely, that at the mouth of this river there was a "large town" [un gran pueblo], should be of itself sufficient evidence that the river was not the Mississippi; for all the other accounts from the early period go to show that the land about the mouths of the Mississippi was practically uninhabited, one may say, uninhabitable. Furthermore, Pineda is said to have ascended the river for six leagues,[1] and found forty

---

[1] Professor Fiske, in spite of the fact that a number of authorities give this limit, says:—"How far he ascended it is not clear."

pueblos on its banks. Twenty-four years later the remnant of De Soto's expedition apparently found no towns on the lower Mississippi. At least Biedma speaks of none, and says the Indians followed them from the place of the last victory "almost until we arrived at the sea, so that we tarried nineteen days on the journey." [Biedma's *Relacion*, in Doc. Ined., III. p. 440.] When in 1699 the French under d'Iberville sought a place for a settlement on the Mississippi, they were unable to enter the mouth in their ships, and had to provide small boats for the ascent of the river. They had to travel for several days before finding the first Indian settlement, instead of seeing forty towns within six leagues; and, moreover, they could find no place fit for a settlement of their own nearer the mouth of the river than the site chosen for the city of New Orleans, which is about 100 miles from the mouth. Then too the description of the fertility of the soil, the healthfulness of the climate, and the riches of the inhabitants, points with much greater probability to another region than to the one about the mouths of the Mississippi, which was found by later explorers to be swampy and unattractive. From these considerations it will be seen how very small is the basis on which modern historians have founded their conjecture as to the first discovery of the Mississippi.

We are told by Mr. Winsor that "at the river Panuco," Pineda "had been challenged by Cortes as trenching on his government." Now it so happens that Cortes himself wrote a long letter to the king, during this very year, 1519, in which he gives a detailed description of this visit, without, however, naming the leader of the expedition. But as he calls him the captain of Francisco de Garay, and as we find no other meeting of Cortes with a more important subject of Garay's during that year, there can be little doubt as to the identity of the expedition described by Cortes and that of our modern historians, to which the discovery of the Mississippi under the name of Rio del Espiritu Santo is ascribed. Some of Cortes' letters are printed in the original in Barcia, *Histo-*

riadores Primitivos; and an English translation is given by George Fulsom, published in New York in 1843; so that the material is accessible to the public. Instead of meeting at Panuco, as Mr. Winsor says, the interview between Cortes and these explorers of Garay took place at Vera Cruz, according to Cortes' own account, who may be supposed to have known. At the "City of Cempoal," four leagues from Vera Cruz, Cortes heard of the arrival of the ships of Garay in the harbor of Vera Cruz, and returned hither for the purpose of learning their mission. He did not see Pineda, or whoever was the captain of the fleet; but his first interview was with a notary and two witnesses, who came in Garay's name to demand a division of the territory. By strategy, Cortes later made prisoners of four others from the fleet, two cross-bowmen and two musketeers; which fact being observed from the vessels of Garay they put to sea at once. These men told Cortes, as he relates to the king, that this expedition had been sent out by Francisco de Garay, Governor of the Island of Jamaica, and had come for purposes of discovery; that they had arrived at a river, "thirty leagues along the coast, after passing Almeria," where they had traded with the Indians, and had bartered for 3000 "Castellanos" of gold; that they had not landed, but had seen certain villages on the shore; that the lord of this river was—PANUCO!

It is a well known fact that the rivers and regions of America often received from the Spaniards the names of the chiefs whom they found in power there. That Cortes so applied the name of the chief in this case is shown by the fact that in paragraph LV of the same letter, when referring again to this expedition, he speaks of the "Rio de Panuco." In paragraph XLVII he says further that the expedition returned to Panuco, after having been at Vera Cruz. Letter IV, written October 15th, 1524, makes further mention of this river as follows:—"I have already given your Majesty an account of the river Panuco, fifty or sixty leagues distant from Vera Cruz along the coast, to which the ships of Fran-"

10

"cisco de Garay had made several visits, when they met with a
rude reception from the natives, on account of the bad management of the captains in trading with them. Subsequently,
when I saw that there was a deficiency of harbors along the
whole coast of the North Sea, and no one equal to that
afforded by the river in question,—I determined to send there."
Garay himself actually came afterwards to Mexico, and offered
to arrange with Cortes, by a marriage connection, the division
of that part of the country. In a later paragraph of the same
letter, Cortes remarks:—"Nothing seems to remain but to
explore the coast lying between the river Panuco and Florida,
the latter being the country discovered by the Adelantado
Juan Ponce de Leon ; and then the northern coast of Florida
as far as the Baccallaos." Now as five years had passed since
Pineda's voyage, on which he is said to have discovered the
Rio del Espiritu Santo, which is believed by so many to have
been the Mississippi, and as Cortes was now in friendly
relations with Garay, in whose employ Pineda had been ; if
that discovery had been the Mississippi, with all the accom-
paniments of fertility, fine climate, and wealth, with which
modern writers adorn it; then why did Garay so much desire
possession of the region of the Panuco? why had he taken so
much pains to conciliate Cortes for it, when he might have
gone to the Mississippi in perfect freedom, even more so
than the French did nearly two centuries later, when the
Spaniards were in possession of all Mexico? why did Cortes
say that the coast between the river Panuco and Florida had
not been explored, if Pineda had been all along it and had
ascended the Mississippi an indefinite distance, as Professor
Fiske would have us believe? If the Mississippi were found
and ascended on that occasion, why is there no mention whatever of it, while the Panuco is so frequently the subject of
Cortes' theme, and the ground of dispute with Garay?

There is preserved to us a proclamation of the Spanish king,
dated 1521, which recites the facts of the expedition of 1519,
the meeting with Cortes, etc., and is published in volume II.

of the *Colleccion de Documentos Inéditos*, . . . *del Real Archivo de Indias*, Madrid, 1864. This informs us that more than three hundred leagues of the coast had been explored, after which they turned and entered a river, which was very large and of great volume, at whose entrance there was a great pueblo ; that they remained here more than forty days, repairing their ships, and trading with the natives; furthermore, that the ships went up the said river six leagues, and found forty villages on either bank ; and, to clinch the matter, and prove the identity of this river with that mentioned by our modern historians, it is also recited that this province is called Amichel. [p. 560.] We are further informed that it was a good land, peaceful and healthy, with plenty of provisions and fruits, and other things of commerce; that there was fine gold, and that the inhabitants wore many ornaments of gold in their noses, ears, and on other parts of their bodies. Here we have evidently the original authority used by Navarrete himself.

We possess also the evidence of still another contemporary writer, who lived in Spain from 1487 almost all the time until his death in Granada in 1526, and who was personally acquainted with many of the leading explorers of that age. It is scarcely necessary to add that we refer to Peter Martyr. He goes somewhat into detail in relating this matter, and makes Garay himself the principal actor, although we know from Cortes, and from the king's proclamation that this was not the case. From Lok's translation, we extract the following passage, as containing the substance of the whole matter. "Garaius sayling to those shores, light upon a riuer, flowing into the Ocean with a broade mouth, and from his ships, discryed many villages couered with reedes. A king whose name is Panuchus possesseth both sides of that ryuer, from which the country also is called Panucha." [Decade V. Chap. I. p. 176.] In the VIII. decade, Chapter II. we find the following account of the River Panuco. "Vppon the banks of this great riuer Panucus, not far from ye mouth, which conueyeth the waters thereof into the sea, stoode a great towne of the" "same name, consisting of 14000. houses of stone for the most part. . . . Shippes of burden may come vppe the channell of this ryuer for many myles together. The people of this Province overthrewe Garaius twice." [p. 285.]

We have the evidence of still another to prove that the great river discovered by Pineda was not the Mississippi, who, though not a contemporary, had such unusual facilities for arriving at the truth of what he wrote, that his evidence on any such point is of value. In the General History of America by Antonio de Herrera, translated by Captain John Stevens, we find that word was brought Cortes that there " was a Ship come from the Northward, having run along the Coast of Panuco, and barter'd for Provisions, and about the Value of three thousand Pieces of Eight in Gold ; that the Men did not like that Country ; that they were sent by Francis de Garay, from Jamaica, under the Command of Captain Alonso Alvarez Pineda." . . . " The seven Men belonging to Garay informed him [Cortes] that they had sail'd far along the Shore in Quest of Florida, and touch'd at a River, and Province whose Lord was call'd Panuco, where they found some Gold, but little, and barter'd, without going ashore, for the Value of three thousand Pieces of Eight, and a considerable Quantity of Provisions." [Book IV. chap. I. vol. 2, p. 238–39.]

This account of Herrera is really the cement which serves to bind the varying contemporary accounts together ; for we have the expedition described in such a manner as to show that it must be the same as the one of which Cortes speaks ; and we have the captain named whom Garay had placed at its head, Pineda, the man who is said to have discovered the Mississippi this same year ; here too we find the terms " coast of Panuco " and " Panuco the lord of the country " ; we have the interview of Cortes with seven men, which agrees with Cortes' own recital, of the notary with two witnesses, and the four afterwards taken prisoners ; then too the " 3000 Castellanos " for which they traded with the Indians in the one case are evidently the same as the " 3000 Pieces of Eight " for which they bartered in the other. The name "Amichel" seems to be known only to the king, of all the contemporary authorities; but if Amichel were other than the region about the Panuco, or in other words, if it were the country of the Mississippi, why did Garay never seek it, instead of returning so many times to the Panuco?

Now in all these early authorities on the voyage of Pineda, I entirely fail to find mentioned his discovery and naming of the Rio del Espiritu Santo. They all agree as to one fact, namely, that he discovered a large river; but when that river is named, the name is Panuco, and not Espiritu Santo. It is true that the royal proclamation calls the territory Amichel; but the description of the great town at the mouth, and other villages on its banks, with the fine climate, the gold of the country, etc., tallies so well with others' description of the region about the Panuco, that it is scarcely to be supposed that two different countries were meant.

As to the name Rio del Espiritu Santo, I have found it mentioned but once by any of these contemporary authorities, namely, by Peter Martyr, in the VIII. Decade, Chapter III. as follows: — "This Alguazill [an intimate of Garay's] addeth many things, not to be omitted. That *Panucus* and the riuer of *Palmes* breake forth into the *Ocean* almost with the like fall, and that the mariners get fresh & potable waters of both, nine myles within the sea. The third riuer, which our men call the riuer of the Holy Ghost [Espiritu Santo] neerer to ye country of Florida, hath a more streight & narrowe channell, yet very rich & fruitfull countryes lying about it, & well replenished with people." One would scarcely interpret this description as showing the first indication of the great Mississippi. Its "more streight & narrowe channell" does not agree well with the "vast serpentine channel" of Elysée Reclus; any more than the "rich & fruitfull countryes lying round about it" do, with the "sterile land" reached by de Vaca, or the "unpeopled island" found by the remnant of De Soto's followers at the mouth of the Mississippi. Peter

Martyr evidently did not confound the River Panuco with the Rio del Espiritu Santo; but he seems to have regarded the former as of the greater importance. Even supposing, then, for the sake of argument, that the river of "Amichel" of the royal proclamation were the Rio del Espiritu Santo of Peter Martyr, there is no good ground for thinking that it was our Mississippi. Furthermore, both the Panuco and the River of Palmes are mentioned as keeping the water fresh far out to sea, a characteristic usually ascribed only to the Mississippi, of the rivers flowing into the gulf; while of the Espiritu Santo, no such remark is made.

Both on the maps and in the later histories and relations, there is to be found frequently the name of the bay of Espiritu Santo. A natural supposition seems to be that the Rio del Espiritu Santo would flow into that bay. Pineda's halting place does not appear to have been on a bay, certainly not on a prominent one. On the other hand, the bay where De Soto landed was named Espiritu Santo; but that was probably the present Tampa Bay, and could therefore have no possible connection with the Mississippi River. The same name was given to the bay where La Salle landed in 1685, supposing himself to have found one of the mouths of the Mississippi, while he was actually on the coast of what is now Texas. In the memoir of Daniel Coxe, an English explorer of the early part of the eighteenth century, and published by French in his Louisiana Collections, the Espiritu Santo Bay is mentioned several times; and from the context, it is quite certain that the writer does not always mean the same body of water. In one place he says : "There falls out of the Meschacebe [Mississippi] a branch which after a course of one hundred and sixty miles empties itself into the N. E. end of the great Bay of Spirito Santo." [Pt. II. p. 233.] This is probably the Amate, which leaves the Mississippi and, flowing through lakes Maurepas, Ponchartrain, and Borgne, empties into the St. Louis Bay. He then goes on to say that there are only two large rivers between the peninsula of Florida and the

Mississippi :—"the first, that of Palache, the true Indian name, by the Spaniards called the river of Spirito Santo, or of Apalache, adding an A, after the Arabian manner, from which a great part of their language is derived ; . . . .This river enters the Gulf of Mexico about 100 miles from the Cod of the Bay of Palache, at the northwest end of the Peninsula of Florida." Now as it is 350 miles or more in a straight line from the Mississippi to the Apalache Bay, it is not to be presumed that Coxe meant the same body of water in these two descriptions. He informs us in another passage that the Coussa [Coosa] River, a branch of the Mobile, "enters the Gulf of Mexico, about fifteen leagues to the west of the great Bay of Nassau or Spirito Santo. . . . The river runs into a kind of lagoon or bay. . . . Near the mouth of this river the French have lately made a new settlement, called Fort Louis. . . . The distance between this river and that of Palache or Spirito Santo to the east is about 190 miles." [*Ibid.*, 235–236.] "The Bay of Nassau or Spirito Santo is made by four islands, which run almost due south, a little inclining to the west." [p. 237.] This last description points rather to Apalachicola Bay, than to Apalache Bay; and as the former receives the waters of a much larger river than any flowing into Apalache Bay, it is possible that the Apalachicola River was sometimes known by the name Espiritu Santo. The nature of the stream and of the country about its mouth agrees much better with Peter Martyr's description of the Rio del Espiritu Santo than that of either the Mobile or the Mississippi. Furthermore, Apalachicola Bay is one that would be very noticeable to an explorer, feeling his way, without a chart, along the shores of the Gulf of Mexico.

In describing the Coosa River Captain Coxe writes :— " Many rivulets uniting, after a course of eighty miles, form a river bigger than the Thames at Kingston, making several delicious isles, some three or four miles long, and half a mile broad ; . . . The first considerable town or province is Chiaha, famous for its pearl fishing." [French, *Coll.*, Pt. II. p. 234.]

Mr. Buckingham Smith's translation of the "Relation of the conquest of Florida, presented by Luys Hernandez de Biedma in the year 1544 to the King of Spain in Council," mentions a town of "Chiha" which the De Soto exploring company reached in four days' march from the ridges where were found the head waters of the Espiritu Santo. "From there we marched four days, and arrived at a town called Chiha, which is very plentiful in food. It is secluded on an island of this river of Espiritu Santo, which, all the way from the place of its rise, forms very large islands." [*Ibid.*, p. 241.][1] Both authors agree that the place mentioned (Chiha or Chiaha) was near the province of Coosa. If we consider that Biedma specially calls attention to the "Apalache, a river dividing the one from the other Province," the probability seems to be very strong that Captain Coxe was in error in applying the name Santo Spirito to the Apalache [Apalachicola]. In the great work of Garcilaso de la Vega on De Soto's conquest of Florida, I have been unable to find that he ever mentions the Rio del Espiritu Santo, though he often makes reference to the bay where the company landed, and where the ships remained for some time awaiting orders, under the name Espiritu Santo. Biedma, on the other hand, makes frequent mention of the river of that name, and among other passages there is one to which especial attention may well be drawn, as it is apparently the authority for the statement generally made that De Soto expected his ships to meet him at the mouth of the Mississippi. De Soto commissioned Francesco Maldonado to return to Cuba for supplies, etc., "and if within six months' time he should hear nothing of us, to come with the brigantines, and run the shore as far as the River Espiritu Santo, to which we should have to resort." [p. 236.][2] Previous to this, Maldonado had been sent on a two months' cruise along the coast, and, according to Biedma, continued "until he arrived"

---

[1] See the original Spanish, *Doc. Ined.*, III. 422–423.

[2] Original in *Doc. Ined.*, III. p. 418.

"at a river which had a good entrance, a good harbor, and an Indian village on the borders of the sea." [*Ibid.*] Garcilaso de la Vega goes into this whole subject much more in detail than Biedma, and as a careful historian and a contemporary of De Soto, his testimony is probably as trustworthy as that of Biedma. He gives the details of the coasting of Maldonado in search of a fine harbor, the latter's report of his success, the orders of De Soto as to his return [in about eight months instead of six, February to October], the account of that return, and the disappointment felt at not finding De Soto, the reasons for De Soto not carrying out his original plan and meeting Maldonado there, and the searches for the missing explorers in the two years following, until at last the fate of the expedition was heard of in Mexico. In all these instances the name Espiritu Santo does not occur a single time as the place of proposed meeting, but another name is mentioned, and always the same name which is *Achusi*. This is always spoken of as a " Puerto " or port, and is described in a manner to remind one much more of a broad river mouth or bay than of any of the mouths of the Mississippi.

That Achusi was not unknown to Biedma, who was one of the explorers, is shown by the fact that he mentions, on the way to Mavila, coming " to a river, a copious flood, which we considered to be that which empties into the Bay of Chuse." [p. 242.] On this river was Mavila [Mobile] forty leagues from the sea, according to the Indian story. [p. 242.] As Mavila was on the river emptying into the Chuse (Achusi), according to one author, and as Maldonado was to return to Rio del Espiritu Santo, according to the same author, or to Achusi, according to the other writer, is it not reasonable to suppose that they were using different names for the mouth of the same river, especially as one name, Mavila, a city on that river, remains fixed? Here, I believe, we have the river generally known as the Rio del Espiritu Santo among the Spaniards. That there was at times confusion, even among them, there is little doubt; but that in general the present

Alabama and Mobile rivers were called by the name Rio del Espiritu Santo, seems extremely probable, if not absolutely certain.

If the reader is not yet convinced, there are many other evidences pointing to the same solution of the difficulty. Having shown what river was probably intended under the name Espiritu Santo, it remains to point out why the Mississippi was not the river thus designated ; for he who contends against a generally accepted thesis must be prepared to show sufficient cause for his non-belief. It has been already shown that the river which Pineda entered and which is said to have been named by him the Espiritu Santo, could be taken for the Mississippi only by doing violence to the best evidence on the matter which we can find. Chronologically, Cabeza de Vaca is the next in order who is said to have discovered the mouth of the Mississippi ; but if he did, he fails to give us the name Espiritu Santo, or any other for it ;[1] so does not need to detain us. Following him, came De Soto, whose name is indellibly enrolled in the annals of the mighty stream, in whose waters his earthly remains were sunk to their last rest. That he did not know the Mississippi under the name Espiritu Santo, at any rate during the early part of his wanderings, has been shown to be very probable, by the fact that the latter name was often applied by him and his followers to a much smaller stream, far to the east of the Mississippi. According to the work of his great historian, he never knew it at any time under that name ; but there is a passage in the memoir of Biedma which gives some ground for assuming that these two names were applied to one and the same river by the men of that ill-fated expedition. Relating their arrival at the town of Quizquiz, he says : " The town was near the banks of the River Espiritu Santo." [p. 249.] However, from that time on, we do not find that he makes any mention of the Espiritu Santo; but he speaks often

---

[1] Shea's *Miss. Valley*, p. x.

of the Rio Grande, though without any connection which makes it probable that he intends the same river. On page 256, however, he mentions "the Rio Grande, from whence we came," in a manner implying strongly that he thereby intended the river near which was situated the town of Quizquiz. From the contemporary relation of the same expedition by a Gentleman of Elvas, we learn that Quizquiz was near the Rio Grande. [Buckingham Smith's Translation, p. 101.]

When we call to mind that Biedma in his memoir never afterwards refers to the Rio del Espiritu Santo, and constantly mentions the Rio Grande; and when we consider that De Soto knowingly went farther west than the place of meeting Maldonado, agreed upon, *i. e.* according to Biedma the Espiritu Santo, is it not reasonable to suppose that in this one instance there was a slip of the pen? since his statement does not seem to be supported by any other assertion either of himself or of other contemporary chroniclers.

For nearly a century and a half after De Soto's unsuccessful attempt to conquer the valley of the Mississippi, this vast stretch of country received but little attention from Europeans; and when, toward the close of the seventeenth century, it again came into prominence, it was first approached from the land side, and not from the Gulf of Mexico. In following the narrative of the explorations and early settlements of the French in this quarter, it will be found that they identified the Mississippi with a number of names of rivers which appear on old Spanish maps, but very rarely with the Rio del Espiritu Santo. Through these men we learn that a number of names were given to the Mississippi, even by the Indians living upon its banks; but the one which has taken precedence of all others is that which De Soto seems to have found in use on the part which he touched, and which the Spaniards translated into the Rio Grande of their native tongue, but which the French retained in what they

understood to be its original form, Mississippi.[1] The first of
Frenchmen to learn of the existence of this mighty stream
and call the attention of his fellow-countrymen to it was
Claude Allouez, founder of a number of missions, and the
first of missionaries to meet the Sioux Indians. [Winsor, *Nar.
and Crit. Hist.*, IV. 286.] This was toward the close of the
third quarter of the seventeenth century. The announcement
of this news inspired the expedition of Joliet and Marquette,
who, however, did not reach the mouth of the river. By Mr.
Neill we are told that Joliet called the river Buade, [Winsor,
IV. 178], while Mr. Winsor himself says he called it Colbert
[IV. 206]; but neither of them affirms or intimates that he
took it for the Rio del Espiritu Santo of the Spaniards. To
the intrepid de La Salle we owe the first descent of the Mississippi to its mouth, together with trustworthy scientific
observations; and he makes the statement in a letter which
has been preserved to us that "this [River] Escondido[2] is
certainly [the] Mississippi." [Margry, *Mémoires et Documents*, II. 198.] (Cet Escondido est assurement Mississippi.)
Thomassy, in his *Géologie de la Louisiane*, quotes the Relation
of Père Zenobe as authority for the statement to the effect
that they found the mouth of the Mississippi "at the place
where the maps show the Rio Escondido." [p. 18.] The

---

[1] According to Shea's *Mississippi Valley*, p. xxiii–xxiv, the word first
appeared in Father Allouez's Relation, 1666–67, in the form *Messipi*; from
which it was afterwards lengthened, though often spelled with only one *p*
by the French. Another form not unfrequent was *Meschacebe*. We are
told the word comes from the Algonquin language, and is composed of
Missi (great) and *sepe* (river). (*Ibid.*, p. 6.) From a letter of a Recollect,
it appears that the name *Mississipy* was that in use among the Ontaonas
[Algonquin?] Indians. [Margry, II. p. 245.] Other Indian names attributed to parts of the Mississippi are Gustacha, Chucagua, Malabouchia,
Namese-Sipon, Tapata, and Ri. Among the French it received not only
Mississippi, but also Grande Rivière, Colbert, St. Louis, and Buade.

[2] As the word Escondido means hidden or concealed, this name is appli-
cable to the Mississippi, which though so great was so difficult to find from
the ocean side.

same author cites also an anonymous relation of La Salle's voyage, which gives us not only negative evidence that the Mississippi was not identified with the Espiritu Santo, but also positive evidence, by calling attention to the fact of their being distant from each other; or to be exact, to the fact that the Mississippi reached the Gulf of Mexico at some distance from the Bay of Espiritu Santo; for this author affirms: "It [the Mississippi] falls into the Gulf of Mexico on the other side of the Bay of Espiritu Santo, between the 27th and 28th degrees of latitude, and at the place where some maps show the Rio de la Madalena, and others the Rio Escondido." [p. 14.] Furthermore, in a letter describing his second voyage, La Salle himself seems to mention expressly what bay he means by the Espiritu Santo, namely the Mobile. [Thomassy, p. 20.][1]

La Salle's attempt to found a colony on the banks of the Mississippi was a failure, as his pilots missed the mouths of that stream and sailed on to a bay on the coast of the present Texas, into which, La Salle persuaded himself, flowed one of the branches of the mighty river to which he had given the name of his patron, Colbert. But the project of establishing a colony on the Mississippi was not lost sight of in France, and in 1699 the attempt was renewed with better success by Lemoyne d'Iberville. In the account of this expedition, Mr. Davis, another of the contributors to the Narrative and Critical History, identifies the Mississippi with the "Palisado of the Spaniards" [V. p. 17], which was the idea of d'Iberville himself, who was struck, on entering the river, by the appropriateness of the name. [Margry, IV. p. 159.]

Captain Coxe, whose acquaintance we have already made, informs us that the Spaniards called the Mississippi the "Rio Grande del Norte." [French, *Hist. Coll.*, Pt. II. p. 224.] Bernard de la Harpe, who wrote a "Historical Journal of the Establishment of the French in Louisiana," and who headed a

---

[1] It is possible that the parenthesis (celle de la Mobile) may be inserted by Thomassy.

French colony in 1718, refers to the building in 1562 of "the fortress of Charlesfort, at the mouth of the river Cahouitas [Chattahoochee?], or St. Esprit, to the east of St. Joseph's Bay." [French, *Hist. Coll.*, Pt. III. p. 10.] As the Chattahoochee River flows into the Apalachicola, which in turn empties its waters into the bay of the same name; and as the latter is east of and near St. Joseph's Bay, we have here one more line of evidence tending to prove the Rio del Espiritu Santo distant from the Mississippi.

Reference has been made several times to the French interpretation of the Spanish maps, or rather to the river on those maps whose position most nearly corresponded with the place where they found the mouths of the Mississippi. We turn now to an examination of the representations of the Rio del Espiritu Santo on some old maps, and of the Mississippi on some of the earliest maps on which it occurs, to see what light they will throw on the subject in hand.

Probably the oldest map on which the name Rio del Espiritu Santo is found is that reproduced for us by Mr. Winsor in volume II. of his Narrative and Critical History, page 218, and which he entitles "Gulf of Mexico, 1520." On it is represented a river flowing into a broad bay very unlike our conception of what the Mississippi mouth could ever have been in historical times. From the head of the bay, extending into the gulf, is the name "Rio del Espiritu Santo." The editor informs us that this map " probably embodies the results of Pinedo's [*sic*] expedition to the northern shores of the Gulf in 1519. This was the map sent to Spain by Garay, the governor of Jamaica. What seems to be the mouth of the Mississippi will be noted as the Rio del Espiritu Santo." On page 404 of the same volume, there is represented what is supposed to be Cortes' map of even date; and on this map the " Rio del spiritu sancto" appears between two rivers that flow into a prominent bay which has a great offset to the east, similar to the form of the Mobile Bay of to-day. Mr. Shea, in his Discovery of the Mississippi Valley, p. VIII, speaks of a

map of 1521 on which the name occurs, but does not repro-
duce it for us or tell where it is to be found. On the great
Weimar map of 1527 the "R : del spirito sancto" flows into
a great double bay which is by far the most prominent body
of water emptying into the Gulf of Mexico. Ribero's map of
1529 represents this body of water in practically the same
manner and abbreviates the name. Furthermore, both of these
maps call this bay "*mar pequeña*" or little sea, which indicates
that the water was salt; whereas a distinguishing characteristic
of the region about the mouths of the Mississippi, mentioned
and emphasized by a number of modern writers on the subject,
is supposed to be that the water is for a long distance into the
sea, sweet. On Ribero's map the form of this *mar pequeña* is
not only strikingly like that of Mobile Bay, but it is represented as receiving water flowing through several channels
into its northern extremity. An examination of a good map
of Mobile Bay reveals the fact that it receives the waters of
the Mobile River through quite a number of channels. As
the map of 1529 pictures only the mouths of these channels
and does not follow them into the interior, some later cartographers were probably led thereby into the error of representing
several large separate rivers flowing into this bay, they not
knowing that all these channels were united in one, a short
distance inland. In Winsor, II. 219, there is a sketch of
Maiollo's map of 1527, according to which the Rio del
Espiritu Santo flows into a large bay with a narrow opening
into the sea, which is so characteristic of Mobile Bay. On a
map of about 1530, preserved in the British Museum, and
copied for the Kohl Collection, the Rio del Espiritu Santo
flows through about ten degrees of latitude and empties into
an immense bay. On the other hand, there is a map of the
following year by Grynaeus, on which the only indication of
the Rio del Espiritu Santo is a "Rio de Spu," to which no
prominence is given, and which may or may not be intended
for the same stream.

Mercator, the greatest geographer of the sixteenth century, who may be supposed to have been possessed of a fair knowledge of what he tried to depict, gives us on his map of 1741 the Rio del Espiritu Santo flowing into a very prominent bay, which is broader at the north than at the south where it empties into the Gulf of Mexico. An early French map, dating probably from the first half of the same century, shows two rivers flowing into a bay of similar form, and names the more westerly of them " R. de St. Esprit." [See Winsor, II. 224.] On the next page Mr. Winsor gives a map copied from one in the British Museum, of the year 1536, which represents the river of the same name flowing into a bay of like form. Jomard gives the fac-simile of a very large and beautiful map of the world, made for Henry II., King of France. On this also the " R de St esprit " is represented as flowing into the northwest corner of a very large bay which is much broader at the north than at the south. As Henry II. reigned from 1547 to 1559, this map must have been drawn about the middle of the century ; and as we see, agrees in its representation of the Rio del Espiritu Santo with the best Spanish maps of that period. The celebrated Homem map of 1558 gives the same representation of this river and bay ; as does also practically Sebastian Cabot, on his official map of the world. Again, in his great map of 1569, Mercator depicts the Rio del Espiritu Santo in the same manner. The following year saw the publication of the celebrated work of Ortelius, which became the model of so many modern atlases ; and on the American map of this work the Rio del Espiritu Santo empties into the " Baia de culata," or Muddy Bay. John Dee's map of 1580 is of the same character so far as it has regard to the Rio del Espiritu Santo. In the Royal Library of Munich there is a fine parchment map bound into the end of the third volume of the original edition of the works of Robert Dudley, on which the Rio del Espiritu Santo flows into a prominent bay which receives the waters from several channels ; and in this it strongly resembles the Mobile Bay of to-day. This map was evidently in use by some navigator; for it bears an inscription to the effect that the whole territory should be moved 20 minutes toward the north and 25 minutes in the direction of Mexico. In a hand-writing different from that of the body of the map, is an inscription which informs us that "Thomas Hood made this platte, 1592." As this is one of the oldest maps of English make that has been preserved to us, and although a fine production, seems but little known, it seemed to the author worthy of reproduction here for American readers. Likewise the Judaeus map of 1593 represents the Rio del Espiritu Santo as a large river flowing from the north into a great bay, which in turn discharges its waters into the Gulf of Mexico. The latest map of the sixteenth century known to us is that of "Wytfliet," dated 1597; and on this also there is drawn a "Mer qurno" which receives at its north-west corner the waters of the Rio del Espiritu Santo, and a little to the east, the waters from three channels of minor importance. The same idea is followed on the map of America in the Purchas of 1625, vol. III. page 853; also on the de Laet map of the same date, where the rivers, however, are not named, but the bay is called "Bahia del Spiritu Santo." Into this bay flow four rivers; and the same are shown on the map of 1656 by Sanson d'Abbeville, where the westernmost bears the name "Rio del Spiritu Santo."

We have thus seen that for more than a century and a quarter the best maps have with a wonderful uniformity shown the Rio del Espiritu Santo emptying into a great bay. We would not maintain that there may not be in existence maps of this period on which this river is otherwise depicted; but we have consulted those of that time which are universally acknowledged to be the best, and have found them showing a practical unanimity among the geographers of the age in representing the river del Espiritu Santo as discharging itself into a prominent bay and not directly into the Gulf of Mexico. And that bay we believe to be the Mobile; although it is possible that the Apalachicola may have been sometimes

11

intended. As the latter is formed by islands, and really projects into the gulf, while the maps show the Bay of Espiritu
Santo stretching far inland, and with its mouth at the same
latitude with the general coast-line, it seems clear to us that
the Mobile was the bay thus represented.

We now approach the period when the French began their
memorable explorations of the Mississippi, coming first from
the inland, where they had heard of the "Great River" from
the Indians; and, following that mighty stream to its mouth,
found that it divided itself before reaching the gulf; and instead
of entering through a great bay, its waters flowed into the gulf
directly, through a number of channels, all of which were of
such a nature as to obstruct entrance from the sea in ships,
rather than to invite it, as did the Rio del Espiritu Santo.
On approaching later from the sea, the French were compelled
to anchor at a distance from the mouth, under the shelter of
some islands, and carry on their exploration of the river in
small boats. As to the character of the region surrounding
the mouths of the river, we shall later let these explorers
speak for themselves. In the meantime we will follow somewhat further the story of the maps.

On the Franquelin map of 1684 (1688 according to Kohl),
we have definitely the Mississippi discharging itself directly
into the gulf; while the Rio del Espiritu Santo is to the east,
and empties into a bay. However, we are informed by
Thomassy [p. 207] that in 1681 Franquelin had made another
map of this region on which he represented the Mississippi as
emptying into the Bay of St. Esprit; but that the expedition
of La Salle in 1682 showed this view to be false, and that he
accordingly corrected the error in the later and better known
map. In Winsor, V. 22, there is reproduced a map of the
environs of the Mississippi, which is said to have been sent to
France in the year 1700, according to which that river empties
into the gulf through a number of channels, and there is no
sign of the presence of such a bay as that in which the Rio
del Espiritu Santo had been heretofore represented as flowing.

On Delisle's map of about the year 1707, the Mississippi
River is represented very much as we find it now on our
maps, while to the east of its mouths is drawn a bay very
similar to that which we have seen on earlier maps receiving
the waters of the Rio del Espiritu Santo; but here the bay is
provided with its modern name, Mobile. This is as it is
given in Winsor, II. 294–95. Kohl reproduces also a map
of the same cartographer, to which he ascribes the date
1717–1720. On this we find for the first time, so far as I
know, the " R. des Alibamons," whose waters later mingle
with those of the " Baye de la Mobile." Here we are on
truly modern ground; the Rio del Espiritu Santo has disappeared, and the Alibama, not the Mississippi, taken its
place. Of the same date is a map of this region by de
Serigny, with the same characteristics. [Thomassy, Plate II.]
One map of later date, and only one, has come under our
observation on which the name Espiritu Santo occurs in a
connection which brings it into notice here; and that is the
map published with the memoir of Captain Coxe, to which
attention has already been called. Here we find " R. Palance
or Spirito Santo." From its position on the map, this river
is probably the Apalachicola, which seems to be also the river
he intended when he wrote of the Apalache.

What conclusion are we to draw from this accumulated evidence of the maps of two centuries? As long as the name
Espiritu Santo endures, that river is practically represented as
flowing into a large and very prominent bay; as soon as the
Mississippi is known, it is found to flow through several comparatively unnoticeable channels directly into the Gulf of
Mexico. When the name Espiritu Santo disappears, its place
is taken by Mobile, which is known to be but a simple modification of that of Mavila, which was the name of the most
important Indian town of that region at the time of De Soto's
expedition, and situated not far inland from the bay [Achusi,
according to Garcilaso de la Vega, and Espiritu Santo, according to Biedma and most modern writers], where Maldonado

was to meet De Soto with arms and provisions brought from Cuba.

But, it may be answered, is it not possible that, at the time of Pineda, the Mississippi did empty into a bay? for it is well known that it alters its channels from time to time; may it not then have altered more or less suddenly the characteristic of its mouth? Let us now examine the evidence on this point. Geologically considered, we are told that Lyell "makes the probable age of the delta 33,500 years. To this he adds half as much for the age of the river-swamp, making in all 50,000 years." [Leconte's *Text Book of Geology*, p. 28.] According to the opinion of another well-known geologist, Mr. Geikie, " The area of this vast expanse of alluvium is given at 12,300 square miles, advancing at the rate of 262 feet yearly into the Gulf of Mexico at a point which is now 220 miles from the head of the delta." [*Text Book of Geology*, p. 389.] At the rate of 262 feet of advancement per year, the delta, in the 373 years since the expedition of Pineda, would have advanced 97,726 feet, or a very little more than 18.5 miles. A glance at any good map of Louisiana will show that cutting off 18.5 miles of the Mississippi would not by any possibility bring the mouth of that river at the head of a large bay, far inland from the line of the Gulf of Mexico. The fact of the matter is, it would bring us up to a point where the Mississippi unites practically all its waters in one great channel; and instead of emptying into a bay whose head waters were far north of the east and west coast-line of the Gulf of Mexico, as the Bay of Espiritu Santo is always represented, it would have reached the latter at the end of a long narrow peninsula, jutting far out beyond that line. But already in the days of De Soto, the Mississippi had two mouths, if we are to believe Garcilaso de la Vega's history of that expedition. [Lib. VI. Cap. x, p. 249.] And that was less than a quarter of a century after Pineda's expedition. When the French came at the end of the seventeenth century, they found the river divided into three channels.

Panfilo de Narvaez is supposed to have lost his life near the mouth of the Mississippi, from which fate Cabeza de Vaca was saved, to wander about the continent for years, but finally to make his way to the Spanish settlements of Mexico, and to write a journal of his meanderings. His description is however vague, and he fails to give a name to the river where the tragedy occurred. However, long before that event took place, these wanderers "arrived at a bay which measured one league across, and was deep everywhere; and, by what it seemed to us, and what we saw, it is the one they call Espiritu Santo." [Cabeza de Vaca, *Naufragios*, Chap. XVI.] As this was within eight years of Pineda's expedition, the Mississippi could not have changed the nature of its mouth very materially during the interval. Accordingly we must reject either the interpretation that the Espiritu Santo and the Mississippi were the same, or that Panfilo de Narvaez was last seen near the mouth of the Mississippi.

In two contemporary descriptions of the fate which met the survivors of the De Soto expedition, there is mention of the exit from the Mississippi River into the Gulf of Mexico. In one' we read :—"After remaining two days, the Christians went to where that branch of the river enters the sea; and having sounded there, they found forty fathoms of water." [Buckingham Smith's translation of a *True Relation*, p. 184.] "With a favorable wind they sailed all that day in fresh water, the next night, and the day following until vespers, at which they were greatly amazed; for they were very distant from the shore, and so great was the strength of the current of the river, the coast so shallow and gentle, that the fresh water entered far into the sea." [p. 186.] Biedma's account, translated by the same writer, reads as follows, and is of especial interest as containing the assertion that the river empties into a bay :— "We came out by the mouth of the river, and entering into a very large bay made by it, which was so extensive that we passed along it three days and three nights, with fair weather, in all the time not seeing land, so that it appeared to us we " "were at sea, although we found the water still so fresh that it could well be drunk, like that of the river. Some small islets were seen westward, to which we went." [p. 261.] Reading this passage carefully, we find that the only reason that Biedma had for saying that from the mouth of the river they entered a bay, was because for so long a time they were in fresh water. Geologically, we know that it was an impossibility for the Mississippi to have entered into such an enormous bay as that one could have sailed straight ahead therein for three days and nights, even in the most awkward boats, without seeing land. If however we call to mind the fact that Moscoso's party had started on their voyage down the river, taking advantage of a great rise in the stream [Vega, Lib. VI. Chap. xix, p. 263], and knowing also that it takes a long time for those waters to subside when they have once overflown their banks, it is not surprising that they found comparatively fresh water for a long distance from the mouth of the river. But we must not allow ourselves to be deceived by this description into believing that the Mississippi then entered into a fresh water bay.

When La Salle and his party came down the Mississippi, they were in much better condition to take and record observations ; and from their accounts we derive quite a different impression of the character of the mouths of the "Great River." Before quoting any of the descriptions of that expedition, let us remind the reader that La Salle named the Mississippi Colbert, which name was sometimes used by the French, but never gained currency ; as the Indian name, or rather one of the Indian names, Mississippi, seems to have been regarded favorably by the French from the first of their explorations on its waters. Although this name is now often if not usually translated "Father of Waters," the early explorers uniformly translated it "Great River," which the Spaniards also did, as their Rio Grande, the name generally used by them in descriptions of the expeditions of De Soto, demonstrates. A good general description of La Salle's dis-

covery of the Mississippi mouths is furnished by an anonymous narrative of the expedition, extracted from the archives
of the French Marine, and translated in French's Collection,
2d Ser., I. 23–24. "We continued our voyage until the 6th
[of April, 1682], when we discovered three channels, by which
the River Colbert discharges itself into the sea. We landed
on the bank of the most western channel, about three leagues
from its mouth. On the 7th, M. de la Salle went to recon-
noiter the shores of the neighboring sea, and M. de Tonty
likewise examined the great middle channel. They found
these three outlets beautiful, large and deep." In the first
volume of Margry's *Mémoires et Documents* [6 vols., Paris,
1879–1886], there is the "Narrative made by the young
Nicolas de la Salle of the enterprise of Robert, Chevalier,
during the year 1682." In this we find the following description of the discovery of the mouths of this most important
stream of our great territory. "On the following day, M. de
La Salle sent M. de Tonty by the left branch, and he himself,
with ten men, descended the right, where we had lodged. He
left at eight o'clock in the morning. M. de la Salle returned
at five o'clock in the afternoon, saying that he had found the
mouth of the river, and that the river advanced far into the
sea, making a bank on each side; that he had carried his canoe
on the other side of the bank, and that the water which does
not communicate with the river was brackish." [p. 562.]
"M. de Tonty returned at nine o'clock the next morning, and
said that the left branch discharges itself into a large sea, at
seven leagues, where they saw an island. . . . They drank
of the water, which was sweet and muddy, and full of croco-
diles or alligators. M. de Tonty was also in the middle
branch; we ascended the river, and went to pass the night
at four leagues [above], on the left as you ascend. Here
there were small trees, some of which were cut down, so
that the arms of the king might be erected there.—The
day following, M. de Tonty returned. He said that the
middle channel flows into a great sea of sweet water. . . . So"

" we erected a cross, and below it, buried a disk of lead, on which were written these words : ' In the name of Louis XIV. King of France and of Navarre, the ninth of April, 1682, the *Vexilla regis* was sung to the setting up of the cross, then the *Te Deum*, and three shots were fired from the guns. Provisions are failing, and each one has only one handful of maize per day.' " [p. 562–563.] In 1684, M. de Tonty himself drew up an account of the expedition of La Salle, from which we translate the following :—" We did not arrive until the 6th of February at the River Mississippi, which was named Colbert by M. de La Salle." [Margry, I. p. 595.] "We continued our route, and, the 6th of April, we arrived at the sea. The 7th, as this river divides itself into three channels, M. de la Salle was to explore that to the right, I, the middle one, and the Sieur d'Autray, the one to the left. We found them very beautiful, broad, and deep. On our return, the 9th of April, M. de La Salle had the arms of the King and a cross set up and the *Te Deum* sung." [p. 605.] The official report of the occasion is preserved, and also given in Margry, II. 190–191. Translated, it reads as follows :—" We continued the journey until the 6th, when we arrived at three channels by which the River Colbert discharges itself into the sea. We camped on the shore of the western channel, at three leagues or thereabouts from the mouth. On the 7th, M. de La Salle went to reconnoitre and examine the shores of the neighboring sea, and M. de Tonty, the great channel of the middle. Having found these two mouths fine, broad, and deep, the 8th, we reascended a little above the confluence, in order to find a dry place, and one which had not been overflowed. At about the 27th degree of latitude, a column and a cross were prepared, and on the said column the arms of France were painted with this inscription :—' Louis the Great, King of France and of Navarre, reigns the 9th of April, 1682.' " M. Margry has also found and printed part of a letter in the hand-writing of La Salle, from which we translate the following passages :—" The Mississippi, which is scarcely broader than the Loire, even where" "it empties into the sea." [Margry, II. 198.] "Moreover, all the maps are of no value, on which the mouths of the River Colbert are near to Mexico; 2d, because it has its mouths to the east-south-east and not to the south, where the entire south shore of Florida faces, with the exception of that part which runs between the river called on the maps Escondido and the Panuco. This Escondido is assuredly the Mississippi; 3d, on the entire coast of Florida there is but this one district which has this altitude, the remainder of the coast being almost everywhere on the 30th degree." [p. 198.] Still another account comes to us, from which I excerpt a sentence, because it contains a comparison with another well-known river. It is taken from one of the monkish Relations of the period, from which so much of our knowledge of the French in America is derived. "They arrived happily on the 7th of April at the sea, where the mouth of the stream is very nearly like that of the Saint Lawrence." [II. p. 205.] However, the writer must have meant the similarity as to the breadth of the river as it enters the bay of St. Lawrence, and not with the bay itself; for we shall see presently that the mouths of the Mississippi were not prominent and easily entered from the sea, like the Gulf and River of St. Lawrence.

La Salle returned to Canada and thence to France, where he received permission to found a colony in the region he had brought to light. In 1685 he returned to America, seeking by sea the mouths of the great river which he had found from the interior three years previous. We shall translate his own words in reference to this peculiar experience. On the 4th of March, 1685, he wrote a letter to the Marquis of Seignelay, dating it from "The western mouth of the Colbert." He says: " I resolved to remount this channel of the River Colbert rather than return to the more considerable one, distant 25–30 leagues from here, to the north-east, which we had remarked the sixteenth of January, but which we had not been able to reconnoitre, believing on the report of the pilots of His Majesty's vessel and of our own, that we had not yet passed the Bay of Espiritu"

"Santo (that of Mobile); but finally, after having coasted continually very near the land, and with fine weather, the altitude made us remark that they were deceiving themselves, and that the river we had seen the sixteenth of January, was in effect the principal entrance of the river which we were hunting." [Quoted in Thomassy, p. 20.] As we have seen by the descriptions of the mouths of the Mississippi, as they were found by La Salle and his party in 1682, one arm was but three leagues long and another seven. If then the two branches had run in diametrically opposite directions, their mouths could have been but ten leagues apart. La Salle himself tells us that where he landed in 1685 was 25–30 leagues distant from the principal mouth ; and this had proved to be the middle one according to the first exploration. We must admit then, that either La Salle was a great fool or else that he realized that he was not on any one of the three mouths of the river which his party had explored three years before. Furthermore he proved that such was his opinion by starting out later on quite a long journey to discover the stream on whose western branch he thought (?) himself to be. Accordingly, we cannot agree with Mr. Winsor when he writes, " The map in La Potherie's *Histoire de l'Amérique Septentrionale* . . . , called Carte générale de la Nouvelle France, retains the misplacement of the mouths as La Salle had conceived them to be on the western shore of the gulf, giving the name Baye de Spiritu Santo to an inlet more nearly in the true position of its mouths." [V. 81.] For, as we have just seen, La Salle himself wrote " All the maps are of no value, on which the mouths of the River Colbert are near to Mexico." If, however, we take into consideration that, at a number of points, there are streams which flow out of the Mississippi, some of which it is reasonable to suppose had been remarked by La Salle when descending the river, it does not appear so monstrous that he should have hoped, even if he did not believe, that he had landed on one of the branches of that mighty and wonderful stream. Furthermore, we should call to mind the fact that mariners then had no good means of reckoning longitude, and that La Salle accordingly was greatly deceived in the distance his ships had sailed after passing the mouths of the Mississippi.

But La Salle perished at the hands of his rebellious followers, and his settlement was abandoned. Other Frenchmen there were, however, who were willing to undertake the accomplishment of the project in which he had failed; and in 1699 another band of colonists, under the leadership of Lemoyne d'Iberville, sought the mouth of the Mississippi. On the way there, they entered Mobile Bay, where they remained five days. D'Iberville tells us, " This bay is very beautiful for habitation; and a large river, with muddy waters, empties into it, at about the distance of thirteen leagues from Pensacola. At a distance of thirteen or fourteen leagues westward of Mobile, we found a place formed by islands and the mainland, where there is good anchorage and protection to ships against storms. I resolved to leave the ships there, and go with the small vessels to the neighborhood of Lago de Lodo (Muddy Lake), which is the name the Spaniards give to the Bay of St. Esprit." [" Narrative of the Expedition of M. D'Iberville to Louisiana." Dated July 3d, 1699. French, *Hist. Coll.*, New Series, v. I. p. 20–21.] According to this interpretation, the Espiritu Santo Bay of the Spaniards was probably the St. Louis Bay of to-day, which receives the waters of Lakes Ponchartrain and Borgne. There is indeed some ground for this interpretation; and, from the nature of the case, it is to be expected that mariners feeling their way along the north coast of the Gulf of Mexico from Florida to the west would find their way into this body of water. St. Louis Bay receives, it is true, a very small portion of the waters of the Mississippi through Lakes Ponchartrain and Borgne; but it is the Pearl River, flowing into Lake Borgne, which would be much more naturally discovered from this side than the Mississippi; and accordingly, if the modern Bay of St. Louis is the Bay of Espiritu Santo of the Spaniards, the

Rio del Espiritu Santo was much more probably the Pearl than the Mississippi River. But this same explorer informs us that into Mobile Bay flows "a large river, with muddy waters;" so that we may also interpret the "Muddy Bay" of the Spaniards to have been Mobile Bay. Furthermore, St. Louis Bay is a shapeless body of water, with its longest diameter running east and west, and is enclosed on one side, only by a series of islands; while the Bay of Espiritu Santo, on the great majority of the maps, has its longest diameter running north and south, the body of water is entirely enclosed by the mainland, and moreover, has a form so strikingly like that of Mobile Bay, that it seems impossible to reject the natural, unprejudiced interpretation,—namely that Mobile Bay and the Bay of Espiritu Santo of many Spanish cartographers are one and the same.

But to continue with M. d'Iberville's description :—"On the 21st, we took our departure for Malabouchia, the name given to the Mississippi by the Indians, and, with two rowboats, some bark canoes, and fifty-three men, we entered this river on the night of the second of March. I found it obstructed with rafts of petrified wood, of a sufficient hardness to resist the action of the sea. I found there twelve feet of water, and anchored two leagues from the mouth of the river, where the depth is from ten to twelve fathoms, with a breadth of from four to five hundred yards." [pp. 21–22.] "On the 7th, at a distance of about thirty-five leagues up the river, I met with some Indians, who told me that it was yet three and a half days' travel before I could reach the Bayagoulas, and that theirs was the first village I should reach. . . . By exact observations, I found its position was sixty-four leagues from the mouth of the river." [p. 23.] This experience has not much similarity to that of Pineda, who found forty villages on his river within six leagues of the coast. To this it might be answered that the inhabitants may have died out or moved elsewhere in the lapse of almost two centuries between the two expeditions; but to that we respond that the banks of the lower Mississippi were not and are not adapted in their natural state to afford sustenance to a large population. Besides the geological evidence, we have very early historical evidence according to Barcia's account of the expedition of Narvaez and Cabeza de Vaca, wherein he speaks of "the sterility of the land" near which Narvaez was lost. [*Ensayo Cron.*, p. 10.] Also in Vega we read of "the unpeopled island which stands at the mouth of the Rio Grande" [Mississippi]. [Lib. IV. Cap. xi, p. 250.] Margry, in volume IV, gives us the journal of M. d'Iberville, from December, 1698, to May 3d, 1699, in which the entrance of the Mississippi is described as follows :—"On approaching these rocks for shelter, I perceived that there was a river. I passed between these rocks, with twelve feet of water, the sea running high, where on approaching the rocks, I found sweet water with a very strong current." . . . "These rocks are of wood petrified with mud, and become black rocks which resist the sea. They are numberless, rising out of the water, some great, some small, distant from each other twenty paces, a hundred, three hundred, five hundred paces, more or less, running toward the south-west, a circumstance that made me recognize that it was the River of the Palisades, which appeared to me well named, because, when one is at its mouth, which is a league and a half from these rocks, it appears entirely barred by them." [p. 159.] . . . . "At two and a half leagues from the entrance, the river forks into three branches. The middle one is as broad as the one by which I entered, from three hundred and fifty to four hundred toises in breath. The other flows along the land to the south-west, and did not appear to me so large." [pp. 160–161.]

Without going into so much detail as to later explorations, it may be well to refer to the facts as found by some other explorers. In 1721, the bar was found to be about 900 toises wide, with twelve feet of water, and the current "very sluggish." [La Harpe's *Historical Journal* of the establishment of the French in Louisiana; in French, *Hist. Coll.*, Pt. III.

p. 87.] Charlevoix, writing in the following year, says: "The bar has scarce any water in the greatest part of those little outlets, which the river has opened for itself;" also, "The greatest part are only little rivulets, and some are even only separated by sand banks, which are almost level with the water." He adds furthermore, that "it is entirely a fable, which has been reported, that for twenty leagues the Mississippi does not mix its waters with those of the sea." As to the "only mouth of the river which is navigable," he found its breadth "two hundred and fifty fathom, its depth is eighteen feet in the middle, the bottom soft ooze." [French, Pt. III. pp. 179–184.] Sauvole, another of the early explorers, is of the opinion that "The Mississippi River has no current or very little." [*Ibid.*, III. 230.] And still another found the water at the mouth of the river, at least in summer, "brackish." [Dumont's *Memoirs*, in *Ibid.*, V. p. 30.]

From this mass of evidence it seems to me to be clear that the Mississippi has never, in historical times, flowed into a bay. That the Rio del Espiritu Santo did flow into a bay is established by the almost unanimous evidence of the maps, which is strengthened by the testimony of a number of writers. The origin of the name, before the days of De Soto, we have been unable to discover in any of the ancient authorities which have come to our notice.

What then is the result of our investigation?

1st. Modern historians fail to give us the sources whence they have drawn their information as to the matter in hand, except in one case, that of Mr. Winsor, who cites Navarrete. This Spanish authority does indeed bear out Mr. Winsor in most of his description, and especially in his closing statement that the country was named Amichel; but he does not give a name to the "river of very great volume," discovered by Pineda. The name of the country Amichel is found elsewhere only in the king's proclamation, whence Navarrete evidently took it; but as we have no evidence as to its position, the name does not assist us in fixing the river of Pineda.

2d. We have been unable to find any authority among the ancient Spaniards for the statement that Pineda gave the name Espiritu Santo to the "river of very great volume" of his discovery.

3d. Where we do find a name for the river discovered by Pineda, it is Panuco and not Espiritu Santo. This is the name given by Cortes and by Peter Martyr, contemporaries of Pineda, and by Herrera, one of the earliest Spanish historians of American discoveries.

4th. The earliest mention that we have found of the Rio del Espiritu Santo occurs in Peter Martyr; it is not made in connection with Pineda's voyage, and the description contains nothing suggestive of the Mississippi.

5th. From a comparison of the accounts of De Soto's expedition, it appears that the Mobile, and not the Mississippi, was the Rio del Espiritu Santo of those days. One ambiguous statement of Biedma may be interpreted as giving this name to the Mississippi; but it entirely lacks confirmation either in the other parts of the same account, or in other contemporary chronicles.

6th. The early French explorers in this region rarely if ever identified the Mississippi with the Rio del Espiritu Santo, while they did identify it with a number of other rivers, whose names appear on the early Spanish maps.

7th. An examination of a large number of early maps leads to the conviction that the Rio del Espiritu Santo as there drawn was the stream now known in its various parts as the Coosa, Alabama, and Mobile; while it is possible that the Apalachicola may have been intended by some few of them.

8th. The geological evidence, and the testimony of the early French explorers, make it impossible to believe that the Mississippi could have been the Rio del Espiritu Santo of the Spaniards.

Until forced by unsought evidence to doubt the identity of the Rio del Espiritu Santo with our Mississippi, the writer of these pages had accepted without question the usual inter-

pretation.   Drawn on by ever increasing interest to investi-
gate the subject more fully, further study gradually changed
doubt to conviction, but conviction that the old interpretation
was wrong, and that a new one must be adopted.   Whether
the evidence and arguments here adduced are strong enough
to convince historical students generally as to the justness of
the author's conclusion, remains for the future to decide.   He
has at least done what was in his power to arrive at the truth.

WALTER B. SCAIFE.

· JOHNS HOPKINS UNIVERSITY
STUDIES

IN

HISTORY AND POLITICS.

HERBERT B. ADAMS, Editor.

These Studies were begun in 1882. Nine series have been completed, and twelve extra volumes issued.

The set of nine series is now offered in a handsome library edition for $27.00, and including subscription to the current (tenth) series, $30.00. The nine series with the twelve extra volumes, altogether twenty-one volumes, for $43.00. The twelve extra volumes (now ready) will be furnished together for $17.00.

ANNUAL SERIES, 1883–1891.

EXTRA VOLUMES.

EIGHTH SERIES.—History, Politics, and Education.—1890.—$3.50.

I-II. The Beginnings of American Nationality. By A. W. Small. $1.00.
III. Local Government in Wisconsin. By D. E. Spencer. 25 cents.
IV. Spanish Colonization in the Southwest. By F. W. Blackmar. 50 cents.
V-VI. The Study of History in Germany and France. By P. Frédéricq. $1.00.
VII-VIII-IX. Progress of the Colored People of Maryland since the War. By Jeffrey R. Brackett. $1.00.
X. The Study of History in Belgium and Holland. By P. Frédéricq· 50 cents.
XI-XII. Seminary Notes on Recent Historical Literature. By H. B. Adams, J. M. Vincent, W. B. Scaife, and others. 50 cents.

NINTH SERIES.—Education, History, Politics and Social Science.—1891.—$3.50.

I-II. Government and Administration of the United States. By W. W. Willoughby and W. F. Willoughby. 75 cents. Interleaved edition for notes, $1.25.
III-IV. University Education in Maryland. By B. C. Steiner. The Johns Hopkins University (1876-1891). By D. C. Gilman. With Supplementary Notes on University Extension. By R. G. Moulton. 50 cents.
V-VI. Development of Municipal Unity in the Lombard Communes. By William K. Williams. 50 cents.
VII-VIII. Public Lands and Agrarian Laws of the Roman Republic. By Andrew Stephenson. 75 cents.
IX. Constitutional Development of Japan (1853-1881). By Toyokichi Iyenaga. 50 cents.
X. A History of Liberia. By J. H. T. McPherson. 50 cents.
XI-XII. The Character and Influence of the Indian Trade in Wisconsin. By Frederick J. Turner. 50 cents.

TENTH SERIES.—1892.—Subscription, $3.00.

I. The Bishop Hill Colony: A Religious Communistic Settlement in Henry County, Illinois. By Michael A. Mikkelsen. Paper, 50 cents. Cloth, 75 cents.
II-III. Church and State in New England. By Paul E. Lauer. Paper, 50 cents. Cloth, 75 cents.
IV. Church and State in Early Maryland. By George Petrie. Paper, 50 cents.
V-VI The Religious Development in the Province of North Carolina. By Stephen B. Weeks. Paper, 50 cents.
VII. Maryland's Attitude in the Struggle for Canada. By John W. Black.
Causes of the American Revolution. By James Albert Woodburn.
Local Government in the South and the Southwest. By Edward W. Bemis and others.
The Quakers in Pennsylvania, 1682-1776. By Albert Clayton Applegarth.

Other papers will be announced from time to time.

———————

All communications as to publications issued under the auspices of the Johns Hopkins University or Johns Hopkins Hospital should be addressed to The Johns Hopkins Press, Baltimore, Maryland. Subscriptions will also be received, or single copies furnished by the principal booksellers in America and Europe.

———————